KU-215-417

LIVI MICHAEL

Frank and the Black Hamster of Narkiz

Illustrated by Derek Brazell

PUFFIN BOOKS

PUFFIN BOOKS

Published by the Penguin Group
Penguin Books Ltd, 80 Strand, London WC2R 0RL, England
Penguin Putnam Inc., 375 Hudson Street, New York, New York 10014, USA
Penguin Books Australia Ltd, 250 Camberwell Road, Camberwell, Victoria 3124, Australia
Penguin Books Canada Ltd, 10 Alcorn Avenue, Toronto, Ontario, Canada M4V 3B2
Penguin Books India (P) Ltd, 11 Community Centre, Panchsheel Park,
New Delhi – 110 017, India
Penguin Books (NZ) Ltd, Cnr Rosedale and Airborne Roads, Albany, Auckland, New Zealand
Penguin Books (South Africa) (Pty) Ltd, 24 Sturdee Avenue, Rosebank 2196, South Africa

Penguin Books Ltd, Registered Offices: 80 Strand, London WC2R 0RL, England

www.penguin.com

First published 2002
9

Text copyright © Livi Michael, 2002
Illustrations copyright © Derek Brazell, 2002
All rights reserved

The moral right of the author and illustrator has been asserted

Set in 13/18pt Bembo

Made and printed in England by Clays Ltd, St Ives plc

Except in the United States of America, this book is sold subject to the condition that it shall
not, by way of trade or otherwise, be lent, re-sold, hired out, or otherwise circulated without
the publisher's prior consent in any form of binding or cover other than that in which it is
published and without a similar condition including
this condition being imposed on the subsequent purchaser

British Library Cataloguing in Publication Data
A CIP catalogue record for this book is available from the British Library

ISBN 0–141–31428–1

Contents

The Hamsters of Bright Street

*This book is dedicated to Ben,
for critical help and support.*

*But especial thanks are also owed to Ian Hunton,
for guidance through the Spaces Between, and to Liam Casey
for providing the first sketch of Bright Street, and to the
Friends of Frank: Sam Casey, Ellis Hodgkiss, Daniel
Jacques, Toby Kane, Laurie Matley, Philip Rafferty, Sadie
Brown, Natasha Christou and Katy Davies.*

Livi Michael has two sons, Paul and Ben, a dog called
Jenny and a hamster called Frank. She has written
books for adults before, but ever since getting to know
Frank has had the sense that he had a story that should
be told. So here it is, and both Livi and Frank hope
you enjoy it very much.

As you probably know, most hamsters are gentle, timid, domesticated creatures. Easily tamed and house-proud, they need little more than water, a full bowl of food and an exercise wheel to adapt to their small homes. Although friendly, they are rather solitary by nature, and are happy to be left alone to take care of their cages. Daylight makes them sleepy, but at night they will spend happy hours separating their food space from their toilet area, relocating their bedding, and, from time to time, running furiously around in their wheels.

Some hamsters, however, are different. Resistant to being tamed, hostile to handling, they don't really want to be domesticated at all. This story is about one of these hamsters. His name is Frank. He is a golden hamster, one of the kind that came originally from Syria, which is where all domestic hamsters come from (other than the smaller Russian variety who don't come into this story). Frank himself came from Mr Wiggs's pet shop just a few weeks ago, when he was bought by a young man called Guy.

The other thing you need to know about Frank is that he has a motto. His motto is 'Courage', and when he says it to himself it always seems to have an exclamation mark after it like this:

'Courage!'

This is a story about a time when Frank needed to use this motto.

1 Escape!

'What's all this?' said Frank to himself, and his nose quivered as he poked it out of his bedding. 'What's all this?'

A moment later his entire home shook, then began to move through the air.

'Man the food supplies,' thought Frank, and he scrabbled around in his bedding, cramming all the food he had stored there into the pouches in his cheeks. This, as any hamster will tell you, is Emergency Action.

There was a sudden drop in temperature and his cage landed, none too gently.

'There you are, Frank,' said a voice he recognized.

It belonged to the Big Human who had bought him a few weeks ago, lifting him from a

3

warm pile of squirming hamster cubs and carrying him through the cold to live on his own, in a cage that stood on a low ledge, wedged between the television and the gas fire.

'Out you come,' said the Big Human, who was called Guy.

Frank burrowed more tightly into his bedding.

The enormous face of the Big Human called Guy loomed close to the bars of Frank's cage. Guy had hair like a sheep and squares of glass on his face. Up close, closer than Frank ever wanted to be to a human face, his skin was pitted and bumpy and bristled.

'I know you're in there,' Guy said, and Frank felt the smelly blast of his breath.

Then the roof of his cage was lifted right off.

Frank knew what was happening because it had happened once before. It was the Grand Cage Cleaning. Which meant that just as Frank got his cage organized the way he liked it, with plenty of droppings to mark his territory, the Big Human came and changed it all, leaving Frank with alien straw and wood shavings, and a soapy smell, especially around the wheel, that he didn't like at all.

Worse, Frank himself was expected to run round in a little plastic globe thing while all this was going on, bumping into the furniture and getting wedged behind chairs. And although he knew there was a way into the globe because Guy put him in through it, no matter how hard he ran he couldn't find the way out.

So now, when Guy's hand came into the cage to take the lid off Frank's bedroom, Frank ran out on to his platform and down the little ladder to the floor of his cage.

'Strategy!' he thought as Guy's fingers groped after him, and he scuttled into his play area, which consisted of a series of interlocking tubes. When one tube was pulled apart he wriggled into the next, then that one was lifted up.

'Tactics!' thought Frank, and he dropped all the way to the floor of his cage and ran behind his wheel.

'Frank!' said Guy, and he rattled the wheel. Then what was left of his cage was lifted up again. Frank flattened himself to the floor as Guy carried the cage back to the ledge it had come from.

'He thinks I'll come out now,' Frank thought, 'to explore.' And indeed he could still make out Guy's face through the wheel, now almost level with Frank as he squatted, waiting.

When Frank didn't move, Guy's fingers probed behind the wheel and Frank nipped one of them sharply.

'*OW!*' roared Guy.

Frank ran.

The base of his cage was a large tray, and Frank had to scramble over the side. Twice the fingers caught him and he only escaped by using his Last Resort – the Lightning Twist Propulsion Manoeuvre, in which all his muscles contracted at once, propelling him forwards and over the edge on to the ledge on which the cage stood.

'Frank – come back!' shouted Guy.

'No fear,' thought Frank, and he ran all the way along the ledge until he was actually under the gas fire.

Suddenly, Frank came to a gap, where the ledge seemed to fall away. There was cold air in front of him, darkness below, and behind, Guy's snatching fingers.

'Courage!' thought Frank, and down he dropped into a musty, dusty darkness.

Guy wailed as Frank disappeared. Frank scrabbled away from the noise, over fragments of loose slate and brick dust that made him sneeze. He came to a wooden ledge, then a further drop over which he dangled for a moment by a single paw, then he landed, unhurt and alone in the darkness of the Space Beneath the Floor. The blood in his veins thrummed quickly. Here at last was Adventure!

Of course it was dark, but hamsters don't mind the dark, being nocturnal by nature and short-sighted in any case. They run along pipes, or along the edges of furniture for guidance, and luckily there was a big wooden ledge beside Frank now – a sort of plank.

Frank had found the main joist that ran all the way under the front room of Guy's house. There was a pipe running along it too, with interesting scraps of material wrapped round it, and bits of tape. There were wood shavings on the floor which made Frank feel at home, and from time to time he came across funny metal objects: screws and nails and a paper clip. He tested the paper clip by putting it into his pouch, but after a moment or two took it out.

Excited by the different smells, Frank ran backwards and forwards for a while, tugging at the strands of material attached to the pipe, and snuffling at the screws, then he paused, listening to the strange taps and muffled clicks that echo through the Spaces Between.

You have to remember that hamsters haven't always lived in cages. Originally they came from the vast deserts of Arabia where in the middle of the day the sun burned so fiercely that no life stirred, and there was no movement, not even the blink of a lizard. There, in order to escape the merciless sun, they became nocturnal, and burrowed for miles beneath the Trackless Wastes, where men who strayed perished, but hamsters flourished, wild, courageous and free. So now, in the earth beneath the house, Frank felt a different hamster, an older, wilder hamster. Instincts he didn't know he had were awakening, and those instincts were to burrow ever deeper, ever further. But beneath the brick dust and wood shavings the ground was hard, no burrowing there, and when he ran to the very end of the joist there was a brick wall.

As he paused for a while, thinking what to do next, Frank suddenly realized that he was very hungry. He ran his paws quickly over his face and head, then began working out some of the food he had cunningly stored in his cheek pouches, by pushing them from behind.

'What have we got here?' Frank thought, holding each piece in his paws.

A few seeds.

A nice chunk of nut.

Quite a long crust of bread.

And some cheese, from one of the cheese and chutney sandwiches Guy ate every night without fail, and shared with Frank.

Guy wasn't a bad owner, you understand, but he did sometimes forget to fill Frank's bowl with proper food. Instead, every evening he made a huge stack of cheese and chutney sandwiches, and sat in front of the telly with a can or three of lager, watching police programmes like *The Bill* and passing bits of cheese and chutney through the bars of Frank's cage.

Which was all right, Frank supposed, if you liked that kind of thing. But in fact cheese isn't the best food for rodents, and Frank couldn't *stand* chutney, so he had to be grateful for the bread when it came.

He was grateful now that he had packed his pouches with all kinds of essentials for his journey. It was rather like having a picnic. He ate his fill in freedom for the first time in his life, and he didn't know when he had enjoyed his food so much.

It was then, as he sat back and rested after gnawing on a bit of carrot to clean his teeth, that he heard the voice.

'Frank.'

Faint yet distinct, a voice that certainly wasn't Guy's, calling him.

'Frank.'

Frank reared up on his hind legs, sniffing the musty air, but it almost seemed as though the voice was coming from beneath him, from the earth beneath his feet. Frank's fur bristled all over as he heard the voice again.

'Frank.'

His whiskers quivered. His spine shivered. And what tail he had retracted right inside his body.

'Frank.'

It was dangerous, the voice; more than that, it was danger. Danger itself beckoning and stirring the blood, and more, even, than that – something old and sweet in his flesh, in the fibres of his flesh and bones. When he heard it Frank lost all sense of where he was, and even who he was. He could only stand absolutely still in the Spaces Between, where anything might attack.

'Frank.'

11

Frank stood still, as if paralysed. Only after the voice spoke for the fifth time did he manage to wrench himself out of his trance and run first one way, then another, in confusion. But whichever way he ran he seemed to come back to the brick wall, so finally it occurred to him to run along that instead. And when he did this he came to another joist, and where this joist joined the wall there was a chink.

It wasn't a very big chink, barely big enough to poke his nose through, but fortunately hamster bones are very soft, and they are used to squeezing through the smallest spaces. I once heard, in fact, that if you make a hole the size of a pencil a hamster will manage, somehow, to squeeze through it, but I don't know how true that is. Anyway, here was a chink and it definitely seemed to lead somewhere, and Frank's natural curiosity was aroused.

First he poked his nose through and sniffed.

Then he nibbled.

Then he squeezed and pushed.

Then he sneezed because of all the dust and flakes of paint.

Then he squeezed again, back legs kicking furiously. And he sneezed and squeezed and squeezed and sneezed, his ribs hurting a little as he kicked and wriggled through to the back of what he recognized as skirting board. And here he had to bend round in a tight place –

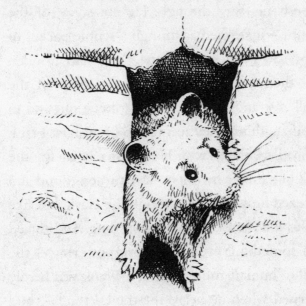

But his luck held, because once he had bent round he could detect light through a crack in the skirting board, and something else – the whiff of a scent any hamster would recognize – another hamster!

But when Frank finally emerged from the crack in the skirting board he found himself in the thickest, woolliest carpet he had ever known. A forest of pink and red strands taller than Frank himself reared over him, many of them covered in dust or fluff and bits of food. Frank found it hard to push his way through. He ate some of the crumbs – it seemed as though a whole packet of crisps had been spilt at one point and trodden in – then he tugged furiously at some of the woollen strands, but they didn't come out and in fact, if anything, they seemed to grow. First Frank was baffled, then cross. If it hadn't been for the smell of hamster he might have turned round and squeezed himself back through the crack, but like calls to like, and the smell was strong. And mixed with something even more overpowering – the smell of human; more than one. Frank was hardly surprised when he heard the thud – thud – thud of human feet, and the carpet trembled beneath him. He didn't know what to do so he cowered down into the carpet (which was at least useful for that kind of thing) and did nothing.

Great footsteps clumped towards Frank and

he crouched down low, his instincts telling him to run. But he knew he hadn't been seen yet, and he was more likely to be seen if he ran. Besides, he knew from experience that humans were terribly stupid. They had practically no sense of smell and couldn't see what was right under their noses. The first time Frank had got away from Guy (which had been on the very first day, when Guy brought him home) he had simply followed Guy around as he hunted everywhere for Frank, in order to learn as much as he could about the new territory. And it had worked very well, since Guy had examined all the likely places, behind ill-fitting cupboards (Guy dabbled a little in DIY) and through gaps in the fabric of chairs, muttering, 'I wonder if he's down there?'

Frank wasn't, of course, he was right behind Guy's foot, and narrowly missed being stepped on before Guy finally noticed. So Frank knew that humans weren't terribly bright, and he managed now to stay absolutely still as the great footsteps thudded nearer.

'Courage!' he said to himself, crouching low, and the footsteps thudded almost all the way up to Frank, then went past, and back again.

This particular human was smaller than Guy and probably female. Frank had no experience of human females but something in the scent made him think he was right. Backwards and forwards she thudded across the room, then Frank shut his eyes as she stood right next to him and let out a deafening yell.

'MUM!'

Frank leaped back and flattened himself into the carpet, his heart going like a tiny drill.

'I CAN'T FIND MY SCHOOL BAG!'

A voice, mercifully faint, came from the other room.

'I thought I'd told you to go to bed.'

'BUT MUM –'

'Tania – it's late. I'll find the bag. Now go on up – I'll be with you in a minute.'

Tania made an exasperated noise then stomped out of the room more loudly than ever. The whole room rattled as she went upstairs. Frank waited where he was and sure enough another set of footsteps followed her, heavier but more weary, a scent like flowers trailing behind.

Cautiously, Frank straightened.

'All clear,' he thought.

The smell of hamster was more powerful now that both humans had gone. Frank struggled on through the carpet until he came to the edge of a chair. The chair was covered in some rough material, much more easy to manage than the carpet, and Frank scampered up it quickly, though once or twice he got his paws caught in loose threads.

Now he was out of the carpet, the brightness of the room was dazzling. Even at the top he didn't have much of a view because he was so short-sighted that it was all a blur, but when he turned round he nearly fell off the back of the chair.

There, quite close to him on a table, was the most astonishing hamster cage Frank had ever seen. Four compartments connected by an elaborate system of plastic tunnels.

Nothing like Frank's metal cage!

There was a wheel, of course, but also a little slide, a special house with windows and a door, a climbing frame and a whole tub full of lovely soft sawdust just for burrowing. There was even a kind of buggy contraption you could pedal.

So taken aback was Frank by the splendour of this cage that he failed entirely to notice its occupant. But when he did he nearly lost his balance again.

There, watching him with fixed intent and a not wholly welcoming smile, was a plump and dazzling white hamster.

The white hamster lay on a kind of cushion of pink bedding. She stared at Frank without moving or even blinking. As Frank gazed back, her lips curled in an even less pleasant smile.

'Well, well, well,' she said. 'And who, may I ask, are you?'

2 The Hamsters of Bright Street

As you have probably guessed by now, the house where Frank lived didn't stand alone. It was connected to a whole terrace of houses in a short row called Bright Street, and Frank's house was in fact the very end one – number 13. Although there were only seven houses on Bright Street, no fewer than four of them contained hamsters. The reason for this comes into the story later.

The houses didn't have gardens, though they did have back yards. At the front, however, they opened straight on to the pavement, and across the road there was a croft, where the grass was tall and feathery, and littered with old tyres and rusty cans. From time to time adults complained about this croft and said it was a dumping-ground, but the children played there happily enough. The road separating the houses from the croft was fairly quiet, though a little further along, standing alone, there was a pub called The Angel, which got noisy on Friday nights.

The first house on Bright Street stood furnished but empty. It belonged to a gentleman called Mr Marusiak, who rented it to other people sometimes, but was hardly ever there himself. There were no pets in this house. Next door, however, at number 3, there lived a sleek brown hamster called Elsie. Elsie belonged to Lucy, who was nearly ten, and who took very good care of her. Lucy kept Elsie in her own bedroom, and had demanded a lock for her bedroom door, mainly in order to keep her brother, Thomas, out. Thomas was a bit enthusiastic where hamsters were concerned. He was given to fits of enthusiasm for many things, especially toys, which he would play with relentlessly for several days and then drop, leaving them broken, or without limbs, and sadly his approach to hamsters was rather similar. So Lucy kept her room locked, when her mother allowed it, and everything inside was ordered, labelled and alphabetically arranged. Elsie's cage was on a wide shelf between the toy elephant and the encyclopedia. Lucy cleaned it out regularly, and changed Elsie's food and water at the same time each day, and whenever Lucy did her homework, Elsie was allowed to roll about the carpet for fifteen minutes in her plastic ball. So Elsie had come to expect a regular, orderly existence, and for her part kept herself busy cleaning her cage and separating her food from her droppings. She was a contented, domesticated creature, who rarely felt the urge to roam, which was fortunate, since the door to Lucy's room was usually locked. Except at night, however, because Lucy's mother had a thing about fire, and being able to get into her children's rooms in emergencies, so even if Lucy went to bed with her door locked, Mrs Keenan would stealthily unlock it a little later and leave it slightly open. Lucy and Mrs Keenan had many arguments about this, but in the end Lucy took to waiting until she was *absolutely sure* that Thomas was asleep, and then she would unlock the door herself, leaving it open the required number of centimetres (two). She couldn't sleep if it was any more or less than this, which was a fact that proved very useful to Elsie, as we shall see.

Next door to Elsie, at number 5, lived a very different hamster called George. George was a sad, harassed little creature with a perpetually worried expression, who trembled, and whose fur came out in patches. He looked quite elderly, when in fact he was less than six months old. He belonged to Jake and Josh.

Jake and Josh were seven and five years old respectively. They regularly had friends round to play at their house (Thomas from next door practically lived there), and their mother, Jackie, often said that she didn't know why it was that every child in the neighbourhood seemed to end up, sooner or later, in her front room.

Now no one meant to give George a hard time, but the fact was, whenever friends did come round, George was the star attraction. Jake and Josh would wake him up suddenly by lifting the lid off his bedroom and seizing him, then they and all their friends would shout excitedly while George made his way across an obstacle course hastily cobbled together from cardboard boxes and tubes, waste-paper baskets, tennis balls and a Lego maze.

'Can he do this, can he do this?' they would shout, and then try to get him to go backwards down a series of tubes by tilting them violently once he was inside. But their favourite game was called Bagging the Hamster. This involved getting him to run around inside their clothing – up one sleeve and down another, or down trouser legs and even into socks. Everyone clapped and cheered while poor George fought his way along all the dark, warm, smelly places that seemed to have no end.

Jackie always meant to see that George wasn't badly treated, but she was very busy. She had three jobs, in fact: at the local Co-op three mornings a week, at the pub down the hill, The Angel, two evenings a week and Sunday lunchtimes, and on Tuesdays and Fridays she did school dinners at the children's school. Even though she did all these jobs she didn't have very much money, but she was the kind of person who always looked smart, no matter how little money she had. She twisted her long black hair into a ponytail from the top of her head, and wore bright lipstick and an ankle chain. She worked hard to keep the house clean, which wasn't easy, as she was forever pointing out, when it was always full of boys, and George's cage did get cleaned regularly and vigorously, sometimes twice a week if Jackie forgot she'd already done it once. The feeding of George was mainly left to Jake and Josh, which meant that sometimes he had a huge pile of food in his cage (cornflakes, crisps) and at other times nothing at all. But the main problem was that Jackie wasn't always around to supervise the boys when they were playing with him. Several times she had come in from turning the back yard into a tiny garden, or from clearing out the attic so that Jake could have a bedroom there like Thomas's, to find that the boys were teaching George to trampoline by holding the edges of a tea towel and bouncing him up and down, or swinging him round and round inside an old sock, or even putting him in the washing machine to see if he could run round inside it as though it was a giant wheel. Once she came in just in time to find them filling the sink with water to see if he could swim (hamsters are desert creatures, as you know, and swimming is not something they do). Each time this happened she got very cross and told them that they didn't deserve a nice hamster like George, and that she would take him to the pet shop so that Mr Wiggs could find him a better home, but the boys always howled so much when she said this that eventually she gave in and George stayed.

As if all this wasn't bad enough, Jackie also owned a large white cat called Sergeant, whose favourite place to sit was on top of George's cage. So whenever George poked a trembling nose out of his bedroom there would be Sergeant's enormous, luminous eyes gazing at him hungrily, and his home was never entirely free from the smell of cat. And Jackie's next-door neighbour, Mrs Timms, was an elderly woman who walked at a funny angle and fed all the stray cats in the neighbourhood.

'Gin and cat food,' Jackie once remarked to Lucy's mother. 'That's all she ever buys. And the whole house reeks of cat wee.'

She complained regularly about the behaviour of the cats at night, when they upset the tubs she had planted in the back yard, and when as many as twelve of them would line up on her back-yard wall ('My wall, mind you, not hers!') and yowl murderously at George through the window. At least that was what he imagined they were doing as he trotted round his little wheel at night, which was the only time he felt was safe to exercise, since Sergeant slept upstairs, on Jackie's bed.

So George's life was a troubled one and there wasn't very much he could do about it, except to manage his food carefully so that it didn't run out, and to hide as well as he could in his cage and hope, every day, that no one would notice him.

Even his dreams were troubled. George

suffered from bad dreams, and from one nightmare in particular, which didn't seem to be connected to either boys or cats, but to come from a Time Before. He always found it difficult to say exactly what it was about, except that there was a whiteness that was not the whiteness of Sergeant, and a suffocating, heavy pressure, and through it all the feeling that the worst thing that could ever happen to anyone was happening to him.

So on the whole it was no wonder that George was balding and trembly though still young. Rather more wonder that he had survived at all.

George lived next door to Elsie on one side and Mrs Timms on the other. On the other side of Mrs Timms lived Arthur and Jean, an elderly couple who didn't have any pets and who didn't want any, thank you very much. Arthur was a short, bossy man who looked after his wife Jean very tenderly (she had arthritis) and he also often did jobs for Mrs Timms, though he too complained about the cats. On the other side of Arthur and Jean lived Mabel, the splendid, snowy hamster facing Frank at this very moment.

Mabel, as you know, was owned by Tania, the daughter of Mr and Mrs Wheeler who lived at number 11, Bright Street. Tania was nine years old and sometimes played with Lucy, though they fell out a lot because each said the other was bossy. Whatever else you could say about Thomas, Jake and Josh, they didn't fall out much. They fought sometimes, furiously, but were generally friends again by the end of the fight. Tania and Lucy, however, fell out for weeks at a time.

Tania was an only child who had begged for a pet as long as she could remember, partly to distract herself from the long and terrible silences that went on whenever Mr and Mrs Wheeler fell out. But Mrs Wheeler was frightened of dogs and allergic to cats, and when they had kept fish for a short while they had all died.

Then one day Tania walked past Mr Wiggs' pet shop and saw a beautiful snow-white hamster.

'Can I have it, Mum, can I?' she begged.

Mrs Wheeler raised all the usual objections, about rodents being dirty, and gnawing their way through everything, but Tania kept up a relentless campaign. She bullied her father until he took her side, and finally persuaded her mother to at least look in at the window of Mr Wiggs' shop.

Mrs Wheeler glanced in, intending to walk straight past. But there was something rather distinctive about this hamster, who sat a little apart from the others, preening itself. It was rather stylish, she thought. But she wasn't going to give in that easily.

'I hope it's not a female,' she said. 'Females have babies.'

'We are definitely not having a female hamster,' she said to Mr Wiggs, inside the shop.

Mr Wiggs assured them that the hamster was definitely not female, and that he could always tell.

Mrs Wheeler glanced again at the beautiful snowy hamster.

'Well,' she said. 'If you're *sure* it's not female …'

So they took the hamster home and called it Magnus, on account of its size and distinction, and a little over a week later Magnus gave birth to ten fine healthy babies. Mrs Wheeler shrieked like a fire alarm when she came down one morning and saw them. She said she would take them all back to Mr Wiggs right away, but Tania cried passionately, and Mr Wheeler promised to help find homes for all of them, and eventually Mrs Wheeler calmed down.

'She'll have to have a new name of course,' she said. 'What about Magnolia?'

Mrs Wheeler was thinking of the flower, but Mr Wheeler, thinking of the paint, said that was a ridiculous name.

'Call it Mabel,' he said, thinking of his Aunt Mabel, the only relative he had who was likely to leave them any money. Tania liked the name, so it stuck. She adored her new pet and brushed her every day with a special powder to enhance the beauty of her coat. She kept adding, out of her own money, to the number of chambers in Mabel's cage, and even sometimes pushed her around the front room in a doll's pram with a flowered quilt.

So these were the hamsters of Bright Street, Elsie, George, Mabel and Frank, at numbers 3, 5, 11 and 13.

They were mainly unaware of each other, since they rarely left their cages. Hamsters (apart from Frank) rapidly adapt to an enclosed life by shutting off the impact of the outside world. The children who owned them played together, so they occasionally caught a whiff of strange hamster on the hands of their owners, but they didn't pursue the matter further. And no children played in Frank's house, of course, so he had no idea he lived so close to others of his own species. And alone of all the hamsters, Frank found himself fretting for the company of his own kind.

Not that Guy was a bad owner or left him on his own for long periods of time. Guy lived on his own and didn't work much, so he had little else to do other than keep Frank company and talk to him, sometimes for hours at a time, about current affairs and political economy, which Frank actually found quite interesting, and astronomy, which he found even more interesting, if a little incomprehensible. Frank, being as short-sighted as the rest of his race, had never actually seen a star, but sometimes as Guy talked he believed he could smell them, or feel them, deep inside. And as I've said, Guy would always share his supper of cheese and chutney sandwiches with Frank.

You might think, therefore, that Frank had little cause for complaint, and in some respects this was true. But there were problems, like getting Guy to remember to change his water, or having his cage turned upside down in a Grand Cage Cleaning, when he'd just got it the way he wanted it. Even the position of his cage was something of a problem. It was quite near the window, which Frank enjoyed, because it meant that if he climbed up the bars he could just see out, but it did catch the sun directly, which he enjoyed rather less. Hamsters in the wild burrow away from direct sunlight and sleep by day. But sometimes the sun through the window of Guy's house kept Frank awake.

These problems aggravated Frank all the more because they reminded him that he wasn't free. He couldn't choose where to make his own bed, or when he ate. No matter how kind Guy was, or how genuinely fond of Frank, he was still an Owner, one of the race that had initially brought hamsters to captivity, and nothing he ever did for Frank made up for this loss of freedom. Besides, there was all the singing.

Guy owned a guitar and sang a lot, sometimes for hours at a time. Sometimes he sang to Frank, which would have been OK except that he often called him a mouse, or a vole, or even a rat, because he couldn't find a rhyme for hamster. But more often the songs went like this:

> *O Frank*
> *You're a treat*
> *You can tell*
> *From the patter of your feet*
> *That you dance to a different beat…*

Most of the time Frank managed to ignore him, but Guy could keep this up all evening, in a droning voice that to Frank was worse than the yowling of Mrs Timms' cats. Frank would stuff bits of bedding in his ears and burrow as far as he could away from the noise, but there was no getting away from it. Which was one of the reasons why Frank had tried more than once to escape. And why, at this very moment, he wasn't in his cage at all, or even in his own house, but in Mabel's front room, facing Mabel.

3 Friend or Foe?

'Well, *hello*,' said Mabel when Frank failed to speak.

'Oh, hi – hello –' said Frank, who was so astonished at finding another hamster at all, let alone such an impressive one, that he had forgotten how to make a formal greeting. Then, as the silence expanded, he said, 'Nice – chambers' (it seemed rude to call such a splendid domain a cage).

'You think so?' said Mabel, and she got up from the pink cushion thing on which she'd been reclining and waddled to the front of the cage for a closer look at Frank.

'– And I'm intruding on them,' said Frank. 'I'd better go.'

'Not so fast,' said Mabel, with just a flicker of

her ruby eyes. 'Who are you and where did you come from? Are you –' she said with another flicker '– a *wild* hamster?'

'No,' said Frank. He had never heard the words 'wild hamster' spoken before, but they moved him strangely. 'My name's Frank. I'm from next door, as a matter of fact.'

'Oh,' said Mabel, leaning back. 'Next door which way?'

Frank told her. 'What's *your* name?' he asked, feeling bolder now.

'Mabel,' said Mabel, with an air of pride. When he failed to react, she said, 'So how did you get here then?'

Frank told her. He found himself getting carried away with the details of his escape and adventures in the Spaces Between, but Mabel listened with the greatest attention and showed no sign of being bored.

'My my,' she said when he'd finished. 'Quite the wandering hero, aren't we?'

Frank didn't know what to say to this so he said nothing. He was beginning to think about leaving.

'What's on the other side?'

'The other side?'

'Of that wall,' said Frank, nodding towards the wall beyond Mabel's cage.

'That wall?' said Mabel without looking. 'Nothing.'

'Oh,' said Frank. 'But you said "next door which way".'

'Did I?' said Mabel, and she turned her attention to a large sunflower seed. Frank began to feel annoyed.

'Well, I'll just have to go and find out, won't I?' he said, and he trotted to the edge of the chair.

'Oh, I wouldn't do that,' said Mabel quickly.

'Why not?'

For a moment it looked as if Mabel wouldn't speak, then she lowered her voice.

'Bad things happen,' she said, 'in the Spaces Between.'

'What kind of things?' said Frank, but Mabel pursed her lips and wouldn't answer.

'Well, I'm off anyway,' said Frank. 'If you won't tell me I'll have to find out for myself.' And he set off down the cover of the chair.

'Wait!' cried Mabel in a hoarse voice, and Frank almost fell off, but gripped the cover tightly with all four paws. 'If you don't know the Thing that waits in the Spaces Between,' she continued, her voice hushed with dread, 'then I can't tell you. But many hamsters go and few return.'

Frank considered this, still clinging to the chair cover. Then he said, 'I'll take my chance,' and set off once more.

'Stop!' cried Mabel, in a ringing voice this time. 'You do not want to know but you must!'

Frank paused again. He didn't know whether this strange hamster had anything to tell him or not, but she certainly looked in earnest. She seemed to be in the grip of a dreadful excitement, and had begun moaning slightly and muttering to herself. After a moment Frank returned to the back of the chair for a more secure footing.

'Well, go on then,' he said. 'What is it?'

Mabel rolled her eyes almost to the back of her head and said theatrically, 'There is a Force that Lures, Frank, and it calls each one by name.'

Frank felt a pang of fear. 'What do you mean?' he said.

Now that Mabel had his full attention she began to move, stiff-legged, from one foot to the other, her impressive girth swaying from side to side.

'Have you ever been Called, Frank?' she said, her ruby eyes glowing. 'Have you ever been called by name in the Dead of Night?'

Frank licked his lips nervously.

'What if I have?' he said.

'Oh, Frank, Frank,' said Mabel, with a deep,

shuddering sigh. 'Few who hear the Call live long enough to tell the tale. Many go but few return.'

Frank felt he'd heard enough. 'What rubbish!' he said angrily, to cover his fear. 'What would you know about it anyway? I bet you've never left your cage!'

Mabel continued to shift rhythmically from side to side, raising her eyes to the ceiling.

'Have it your own way, Frank,' she said silkily. 'I dare say you'll have to meet Him for yourself in the end. They all do,' she added.

'Meet who?' said Frank.

Mabel still wouldn't look at him. She was acting as if in her mind he was already lost.

'Why, the Black Hamster of course,' she said, in the same sweet, silky tones, as if to no one in particular.

'The – *what*?' exploded Frank.

'Do not pretend!' Mabel cried suddenly in terrible tones. 'Do not pretend that you do not know that Name – the Name that every hamster has etched on his heart, that runs in our blood to the very fibres of our being!'

There is a kind of force that comes from

people who are very used to getting their own way, and Frank felt this force in Mabel now. Also, in addition to moving from side to side she had extended her arms and was flexing her paws. First the palm of the right paw was turned upwards and the left down, then the left was rotated upwards and the right down, all in the same peculiar, rhythmical motion, so that Frank, watching, felt slightly mesmerized. He began to feel that he knew what she was telling him, he felt an echo of knowledge in his heart, and the memory of that voice calling him in the deep spaces beneath the floor returned vividly. Unable to run, he placed all four paws firmly on the back of the chair to steady himself and licked his lips again.

'Tell me what you mean,' he said, in a dry, papery voice.

Then Mabel reared up on her back legs and, folding her forepaws on her chest, pointed the toes of first one foot then the other, stepping round her cage in a circular motion without ever taking her eyes off Frank. And when she began to speak it was in a high, chilling tone.

'Long ago and far away, O my brethren, O my kin,' she began, as if there were thousands in the room, not just Frank, 'when hamsters were wild and lived out their barbaric lives beneath the Trackless Wastes, when they were hunted at night by great winged, beaked creatures and ravaged by famine and disease, there was fighting in the burrows and the dam in the den ate her young. Then it was that one or two of our race first saw him. The Black Hamster of Narkiz.'

Mabel's voice sank to a whisper and Frank shuddered at the terrible images invoked by her words. She continued to move slowly as she spoke, in ever-decreasing circles, her eyes wide, her face pale and passionless, her head slightly inclined to the right.

'They saw him,' Mabel went on in the same sunken voice, 'whenever there was destruction or waste. Whenever a hamster strayed into the rocky places where he could not burrow, and was scorched by the merciless sun, he was there. When talons swooped, when young died, when a solitary hamster lapped at a poisoned pool, there was he. Where there was disease and madness, and young bucks fought to the death, there was the Black Hamster of Narkiz.'

Now the name Narkiz meant something to Frank, though he couldn't have said precisely what. In fact it was the name hamsters use for their ancient territory beneath the Syrian sands; a name passed from one generation to the next since prehistoric times. Frank may have heard it from his own mother, or it may have lurked in that part of his memory which in hamsters is particularly strong, and which is not merely personal but collective, containing the memory of the whole race.

Mabel was moaning as she stepped from side to side to give time for Frank's collective memories to unfold.

'Of course most who saw or heard him were lost,' Mabel continued in a monotonous singsong this time. 'Yet one or two witnessed and were able to escape, or reported hearing his voice before going mad and running into the wild. For the Black Hamster is a Force that Lures, and one by one the members of our tribe were picked off. But when the Elders realized the full extent of what was happening, a great Council was held. For days debate raged back and forth beneath the sands until finally a decision was made.'

Mabel extended her forepaws wide at this point, the right paw facing upwards and the left down, and she went on in the same hypnotic monotone.

'There was in our territory a new predator called Man. When I say new, of course, I mean he had only been around in the last hundred thousand years or so — for what is that to the ancient race of hamster, that has seen the Ages of the World come and go? However, for most of its existence Man had been little more than a scavenger, wandering in the desert without sense or skill, eating waste that even the vultures left, then dying. But in later centuries Man became more organized. And most recently, our spies reported that Man was trying not merely to prey on other creatures, but to learn from them, to contact them and keep them safe. As though the race of Man was finally acquiring wisdom, so our spies said. And so finally at the Council a desperate plan was made. In order to save the race of hamster, volunteers would *allow themselves to be caught.'*

Mabel's eyes were huge and Frank couldn't move.

'Imagine the danger,' she breathed, 'of being caught by the wrong kind of human. Imagine the danger of just surfacing at all. But that was what the Council required – volunteers to give up their lives for the greater good. Many were lost, carried off by desert creatures or by the wrong type of Man. Many, many times Man simply walked by without noticing the presence of a small determined creature trying to attract his attention.'

(Frank knew what that was like from his experiences with Guy.)

'But at last a Man was found who saw. He was found by a mother with her young – a large litter, twelve in all. Great was the rejoicing when our scouts reported that all thirteen had been taken in the name of Science, with the aim of Breeding. Our goal was accomplished. Let the Black Hamster do his worst, we had ensured the survival of our species. Ever since that day, thirteen has been our sacred number.'

Mabel sighed dreamily and was silent.

'But what happened to the others?' said Frank, when he could speak.

Mabel's expression barely changed. 'Lost, of course,' she said as though Frank should have known. 'I just told you they were a doomed race. You don't think the Black Hamster would give up until he'd got every man-jack of them, do you? No. His thirst is never slaked.'

'But – what *is* he?' said Frank, dashing away a tear, for to him this news was terrible. 'Surely one of our race might have fought him? I would have done,' he went on wrathfully. 'Or why couldn't the whole pack set on him at once?'

'Have you not listened?' thundered Mabel. 'The Black Hamster is not to be attacked or defeated. He is not flesh or blood or bone like an ordinary hamster. He is older than that, much older. He is the oldest thing the world knows,' said Mabel, her voice sinking again. 'He destroys everything, but is himself indestructible. Without beginning, without end. And we thought we had saved ourselves, but we should have known.

Worse was to come.'

Frank trembled.

'The breeding programme succeeded, yes,' Mabel whispered, 'beyond the wildest expectations of the Elders. Soon there were thousands of hamsters the world over, thriving in captivity – all from the original thirteen. But soon the rumours began, that even in captivity he came, seeking the weak, the foolish, the vulnerable, and calling them by name. In the dead of night he comes, to lure them to the Dark Places and beyond, even to the Pits of Doom!'

Frank shivered but Mabel went on, her voice rising.

'Darker than the darkest night is he, and his voice is like the whisper of the earth. And only when he has lured you will he show himself, his red eyes, his bloody fangs – *aiyee!*'

Mabel finished on a shriek and Frank shut his eyes and clapped his paws over his ears, nearly falling off the chair. 'Courage!' he managed to say to himself over the drumming of his heart, but in a very weak, faint voice.

'How do I know,' he managed to say at last,

'that any of this is true?'

Mabel smiled her malevolent smile.

'Oh, I think you know it,' she said. 'Yes, I think you do. All our tribe knows it, Frank,' she added sweetly. 'Especially you.'

Frank felt a terrible pang of fear, but he wouldn't entirely give up.

'I don't believe you,' he whispered. 'You're making it up.'

Mabel turned on him with a look of blistering contempt.

'Then,' she said, 'you are already doomed and you don't even know it.'

Frank ran.

Right down the side of the chair to the carpet, where he struggled through, followed by the sound of Mabel's high, unnerving laughter. Fortunately the track of his own scent was still strong and he was able to follow it all the way to the crack in the skirting board, where he pushed and kicked and kicked and pushed his way through to the other side. There at last he was away from Mabel, her terrible words, her powerful scent, but now, in the darkness, a kind of panic seized him, and he ran furiously along the joist without pause, all the way through the Spaces Between. Not daring to stop and sniff, to listen or even think, he ran on until there was not a breath left in his body and he had stitches in both sides. Then at last he found the hole down which he had escaped, and he clambered and pushed and scrabbled until finally, dusty and breathless, he emerged on to the ledge beneath the gas fire and sneezed three times.

'Frank!' cried Guy, scooping him up. '*There* you are!'

4 Lost or Found?

'What am I going to do with you, Frank?' Guy went on, raising a squirming Frank towards his face and looking at him severely. 'I thought I'd lost you this time, I really did –'

He sighed and sat down, and Frank could tell he was in for a serious talking-to. He gave in, too exhausted by his long journey to struggle any more, and rested his paws on Guy's thumb.

'That's better,' said Guy. 'Now listen, Frank. This has got to stop. One of these days you'll wander off and you won't be able to find your way back. And then what will you do? You know what happened to Stanley.'

Frank had been told, twice now, what had happened to Stanley, the previous occupant of his cage. In fact there had been two previous occupants, because a year or so ago Guy had taken on an elderly hamster called Duke. Duke had belonged to Guy's nephew, Luke, but when Luke had been given a dog for his birthday Duke had been sadly neglected, and Guy's sister Mary had begged Guy to take Duke on.

'I just haven't got time,' she said, 'with working nights at the hospital. And Jeff's working days. I know he'll be happier with you.'

So Guy had brought Duke home, together with his cage, the little plastic ball for exercising in, several bags of food, sawdust and bedding, and all the other bits and pieces you might need if looking after a hamster for the very first time. Guy bought sunflower seeds in specially, and a book on the care and upkeep of hamsters, and even composed his first hamster song, but sadly Duke, already an elderly hamster, died within the week.

And Guy missed him, though Duke hadn't really been very active. But he had shared a cheese and chutney sandwich with Guy and listened uncomplainingly to Guy's song. Besides he now had an empty cage and all this hamster gear. So after another week of gazing mournfully into the empty cage, and drinking a few too many cans of lager, Guy went to Mr Wiggs' pet shop and bought a large, muscular-looking hamster called Stanley.

Stanley was a bit of a star. He worked out for hours at a time on his wheel and then swung like Tarzan from one bar of his cage to another. Guy wrote several songs for him, and even bought him a mirror for a budgie's cage so that he could preen himself in front of it and flex his tiny muscles. But Stanley was also an inquisitive hamster, and when he found one day that swinging on the bars of his cage opened the door, he climbed out at once. Guy thought afterwards that he might have been trying to get to the bigger mirror on the back wall. But he was hardly half-way across the carpet when the floor began to vibrate and there was a roaring sound so terrible that Stanley could only flatten himself into the pile.

And that was how he met his horrible end – in the vacuum cleaner.

Guy was most upset, all the more so because hoovering was not a thing he ever did. It was his mother who had come to visit and had insisted on cleaning up. Guy never forgave her. And he couldn't bring himself to look at the empty cage this time, so he packed it away. But from time to time he couldn't resist looking in at the window of Mr Wiggs' pet shop. And one day he had seen Frank's nose poking out of a nest of tiny hamsters. Of them all he was the only one who seemed alert, eyes wide open, taking everything in.

Guy had walked past him that time, but the next time Frank had crawled out of the nest and pressed two paws against the walls of the glass tank as Guy walked by.

No, Guy told himself, I can't go through all that again, and he had stayed away from the pet shop for over a week. Then finally, one lunchtime, after having a drink or two at The Angel, he felt he had to check to see if Frank had been sold yet. And this time Frank followed Guy all the way from one side of the tank to the other, and stood up, watching him walk away.

It was too much. Guy turned round and walked right back into the shop.

'Just my luck you turned out to be such a wanderer,' Guy said now. He rubbed his thumb over Frank's forehead and Frank squirmed and flattened his ears. Then Guy lifted him so that he was even closer to his face, which smelt like old pork.

'Try to get used to it, Frank, eh?' he whispered, and Frank saw that his eyes had gone peculiar and misty. It might have been a moving moment, except that Frank was forced to stare rather further up Guy's nose than he liked, and endure the overwhelming smell of his breath (lager and chutney). But he could see, as Guy lowered him gently back into his cage, that Guy had literally turned the room upside down to search for him. All the furniture had been moved, one cupboard taken to bits and clothes scattered in a greater than usual disarray.

As he ran from one part of his cage to another, Frank could smell the distant scent of both hamsters; the frail, elderly smell of Duke, the proud, muscular smell of Stanley, and he did feel sorry for Guy in a way. But soon Guy was offering Frank bits of cheese and chutney sandwich again (which Frank didn't refuse, because he was starving) and getting his guitar out.

> *'Frank, if I lost you*
> *I'd never rest*
> *Till I found your new nest ...'*

On and on he went, in a crooning whine, and all Frank could do was sigh and stand on his little platform so that he could gaze out towards the window, where there was a white blur of moon, and if he stretched upwards he could just see the waving tips of grass in the World Beyond. Out there, he thought, in the Wild.

5 George's Terrible Ordeal

Meanwhile, poor George had been having a terrible time. Jake and Josh had invited their friends round, Jamie and Alex. They had set up the Scalextric and played with it for over an hour, then, when they got bored, they turned their attention to George. Someone (I think it was Alex) thought it would be very funny to put George on the Scalextric track. They set the speed on 'Slow'. Alex and Josh stood by to catch George if he fell off the track, and roared with laughter as he scrambled frantically out of the way of the cars. Then they increased the speed and someone (I think it was Jamie) had the bright idea of putting George *on* the cars as they whizzed round. This didn't work too well, but they used fishing-nets to catch him as he flew off.

Then, when they were tired of this game, Josh found his old paint-gun blaster, and everyone thought it would be a wonderful idea to try to fire George from it on to a cushion.

Fortunately, before the first shot was fired, Jackie came in.

'What are you doing?' she demanded.

In three strides she crossed the room and rescued the trembling George from the nozzle of the gun.

'I've told you before,' she shouted. 'What have I told you? You're not fit to have a hamster.'

Poor George lay curled in a ball in her hands, deafened by the sound of her voice. She was shouting so loudly that he couldn't hear the words, just a noise that sounded to him like the cawing of birds. Then suddenly it stopped.

'Poor little thing,' Jackie said in softer tones. 'Do you want to go back to bed?' And she lowered George gently back into his cage.

'I can't believe,' she said, stern again, 'that I brought the two of you up to treat poor defenceless creatures –'

The door bell rang and Jackie went to answer

it, forgetting to close the lid on George's cage.

'Oh hi,' she said to Jamie and Alex's mum. 'Is it that time already? Yes, they've behaved themselves – they've been fine – don't forget your school bags, boys – *no*, they weren't too boisterous – boys will be boys, eh?'

Jackie's voice ran on as all the boys tried to squeeze themselves through the door at the same time. She talked about Parents' Evening, and the cost of school dinners going up and how fast the boys grew out of their school uniforms, and soon everyone forgot about George.

Except for Sergeant.

First Sergeant crouched, watching the open cage, then he began to creep towards it, his tail twitching from side to side.

Imagine how George felt when Sergeant's enormous white face loomed suddenly over the space where the door to his cage should have been.

'Interesting,' said Sergeant in his silky voice, and he extended a white paw right into the cage. 'Come out, little chap. No point resisting. It's all over now.'

George scrabbled frantically round the back of his wheel.

'I can wait,' said Sergeant, and he gave the wheel a little push so that it pressed uncomfortably against George.

'I – can – wait – as – long – as – it – takes,' he said, and he poked his paw round one side of the wheel, then the other.

Poor George! In the limited space he flattened himself first one way then the other, but it was plain that Sergeant wasn't going to give up and George was already very tired.

What would have happened if Sergeant hadn't suddenly overbalanced, trying to climb further on to the top of the cage, I really don't know, but he did, taking the whole cage with him in a shower of wood shavings.

The crash brought Jackie and the boys running back in. George rolled over in the wood shavings and emerged, sneezing, expecting any moment to be clamped in Sergeant's jaws. Instead of which he rolled right out of the door of his cage!

'Get him!' Jackie cried, and three pairs of feet

thudded towards George across the carpet at the same time as Sergeant pounced.

Jackie seized Sergeant and George ran.

How he escaped he never knew. Probably the Scalextric helped. While Jake and Josh yelled in excitement and fell over cars, George scuttled over the rug and whisked himself under the settee.

It was an old settee and the lining was loose. George had hidden there safely before, but this time Jackie and the boys up-ended it right away.

'I'm not having that hamster loose in this house!' Jackie cried.

George slid, very bumpily, from one side of the settee frame to the other. Then (and here luck must have been on his side) he found a hole in the fabric, and when he squeezed himself through he was facing the meter cupboard.

'There he is!' shrieked Jackie.

Into the meter cupboard went George (fortunately the door never shut properly over the carpet) and clambered past a stack of telephone books.

'Don't let him get to the back!' Jackie screamed.

Too late!

George was already at the back of the telephone books and there before him was a hole the size of a human fist. He disappeared into it just as Jake hauled all the telephone books out.

'Oh, I don't *believe* it,' he heard Jackie lament. 'He's gone now – he's got away!'

6 A Friend in Need

George didn't stop running, because Jake's fingers came through the hole after him. Besides, he had no idea where he was, and if he'd stopped he would have been too overcome by the strangeness to do anything. So he trotted quickly through the gusty hollows, his eyes rapidly adjusting to the lack of light, not daring to listen to the clicks and clunks, the echoes and strange gurgling noises coming from the pipes. On and on he trotted, until he felt ready to drop from exhaustion, and began to think he might die there, alone in the Spaces Between.

Then at last he felt a change in the air. Looking up, he saw a kind of vent with slats in it, and through the slats there was light.

Getting up to the vent wasn't easy, but

George was pulled by the faintest of smells, something he recognized as food. He clambered up, using little cracks in the brickwork, sniffed cautiously at the vent, then sniffed some more.

There, through the smell of food, he could make out another scent, becoming sharper and more distinct – the scent of another hamster.

George clung to the comparative safety of the vent, and only his nose peeped through as the other hamster approached. He didn't dare go forward through the vent, and he couldn't stay where he was indefinitely, and the worst prospect of all was going back; so he stayed where he was as the scent of hamster swirled around like a vapour inside his head until he felt quite faint.

'Who is it?' said a nervous voice, sharp with apprehension; then, as George said nothing, she (for it was a female) climbed up to the vent.

'What are you doing here?'

She was a neat brown silky hamster with a worried expression. When George still didn't answer, she said, 'Well, either come through or clear off. You can't stay there all night.'

George made a feeble effort, but the slats were narrow.

'Try over here,' she said. 'There's more of an opening.'

When George hesitated, she said, 'Come on, let's have a proper look at you.'

What else could George do? He felt his way cautiously along the vent until he came to a place where one slat was missing, or broken off. Here, trembling with fear, he scrambled through without looking at the other hamster in case he panicked entirely. So it was a shock when her voice sounded right in his ear.

'My word,' she said. 'Whoever owns you?'

George actually leaped into the air, and then went into his version of the battle pose, though it wasn't a very good one.

'Very scary, I'm sure,' said the other hamster. 'My word, you're a sorry sight.'

Of course George wasn't exactly looking his best, with sawdust from his cage still clinging to him, and all the dust from the Spaces Between. He had torn an ear somehow in the Great Escape, and scratched himself quite deeply across the back, but it was his general condition that was most distressing, the balding and trembling; the matted state of what was left of his pelt.

'I'm Elsie, by the way,' the other hamster went on. 'What *do* you smell like?' and she approached him, sniffing. George flinched. 'It's all right, I won't *eat* you,' she said. 'Although I suppose it has been known.'

She came right up to George and sniffed all round his ears, while George submitted to this humiliating procedure as though he had no resistance left.

'You smell like – like *kin*,' she said, drawing back in wonder.

George raised his head for the first time and looked at Elsie. And then something happened that is not uncommon among hamsters. They experienced a Shared Memory.

Hamster memory is not like ours. It is more of the body than the mind. Put two or more hamsters together and they will begin to remember shared history or kinship patterns, and even, if left together long enough, the collective history of their tribe. Some people say that this is why they prefer to live alone, getting on with their own thoughts and memories without interference.

But now Elsie and George experienced a powerful Shared Memory, of lying curled up together with a number of other tiny hamsters in a warm space that smelt of old sawdust and new hamster.

They stared at one another, speechless for a moment, then Elsie touched her nose gently to George's.

'It's you,' she whispered, and regarded him with shining eyes.

For they had realized that they were brother and sister, from the same litter!

All this was too much for George, weakened as he was by hunger and bad treatment, and he tottered, almost falling. Immediately Elsie was at his side, nuzzling him into a standing position.

'You need food,' she said, for she was an immensely practical hamster, and she knew she would have to wait to hear the full story. She led him slowly, supporting him, across the carpet to the tiles where the kitchen began, talking all the way to distract him.

'*How* long did you say you've been in the Spaces Between? How dreadful – I shouldn't like it at all – I've never tried – give me a nice warm cage any day – what did you say your name was?'

'George,' George managed to say, and there they were, in the kitchen.

'There's always food under the table when the family have eaten,' she explained. 'Do you think you can manage it, dear?'

George managed. There were specks of rice and breadcrumbs, and a nice lump of carrot Elsie brought over specially for him. She found other titbits too – cheese and cracker and even a chunk of apple.

George ate ravenously and Elsie stood over him tenderly. He only looked up once.

'You're not eating,' he said.

'No,' said Elsie. 'I've got lots of food in my cage. But you look as though you need a good feed before attempting the stairs.'

'The stairs?' repeated George.

'My cage,' explained Elsie. 'It's upstairs.'

'Your – cage?' echoed George rather stupidly.

'Well, where else were you planning to stay? The family are all out now, but they'll be back soon. I suppose you could try making a nest somewhere, but it's hardly safe. I think the best thing is to hide you in my cage for a while. Until you feel a bit better. At least that way you're guaranteed some food.'

It seemed incredible to George that another hamster would invite him into her cage, and he wasn't entirely comfortable with the idea.

'Well, you're not fit to go back yet, are you?' Elsie said, and George shook his head vigorously. He definitely didn't want to go back.

'In fact you're not fit for very much. And in my cage there's water, and a nice soft bed. I'm just hoping you can manage the stairs.'

Elsie spoke very authoritatively, and the thought of water and a bed attracted George as much as the thought of going back repelled him, but he still didn't see how he could stay in another hamster's cage without being detected.

'You just leave that to me,' Elsie said, as though reading his mind (which in fact she was). 'It shouldn't be too hard. Now – do you think you've eaten enough for the time being?'

Elsie led George back across the tiles, explaining as they went that it was the greatest good fortune that they had met up like this, since she would usually be tucked up in her cage at this time, and normally Lucy would have locked her bedroom door, but the family had gone out – Lucy to Brownies, Thomas to karate, and Lucy hadn't been able to find her Brownie beret and had accused Thomas of taking it, and they had argued, and everyone had been late, and Lucy finally had found the beret and had run downstairs without locking her bedroom door. Left alone with an unexpectedly open door, Elsie had started to feel bored and restless.

'So you see it was the most amazing coincidence,' she told George. 'Now – here we are.'

George looked up.

In Lucy's house there was an open-plan staircase with great gaps between the stairs. Seen from George's angle they seemed to go on for ever in an impossible, dizzying way.

'I can't,' he quavered. He had never in his life tackled stairs before.

'It's quite easy,' Elsie said briskly. 'I'll show you.'

At the bottom edge of the banister there was a rail going all the way up.

'This is the only difficult bit,' said Elsie, and she skilfully ascended the stair rod to the bottom edge of the banister rail, then ran upwards along it a little way before returning to George.

'You try,' she said, so George tried, but he did find it difficult. He clambered up a little way, then slid down again, tried again and fell.

Elsie picked him up. 'Stand on my back,' she said kindly.

George had never done anything like this before, but there was no point in arguing, so he climbed on to Elsie's back, slipping a little on her silky pelt. Female hamsters are bigger than males, and though Elsie was quite small she had been well nourished all her life and was strong, whereas George was thin and light. Once he was on her back he found it quite easy to climb on to the rail, then he waited while Elsie got in front so that she could show him how to get past the spindles that were fixed into it.

George followed Elsie, inching his way upwards along the rail and not daring to look down. At last they came to what Elsie called the Top Landing. Here there was a carpet with a very short pile which felt hard underfoot but was easy to run along. George trotted behind Elsie, trying not to question any of the strange noises and smells. They passed one door which Elsie said was the Master Bedroom, where Lucy's parents slept, and another from behind which strange gurgling, watery noises came from something Elsie called the Cistern. Just after this Elsie paused, looking up.

'That's where the Boy in the Roof lives,' she told George. 'You have to look out for him.'

George knew all about boys you had to look out for, of course, but he had never heard of them living in the roof, and when he looked up he couldn't see much, just a vast, shadowy ceiling. He shivered.

'Not far now,' said Elsie kindly, and finally there they were, at the door of Lucy's room. As usual it was only just open far enough for George to follow Elsie through, which he did nervously, because here the smell of strange human was very strong.

Elsie took George to a canvas curtain, which hung down from the ledge.

'Now this bit's easy,' she said, and started to run up it. George stayed where he was.

Elsie paused. 'What's up?' she said.

George couldn't say exactly what was up. Overpowered by the smell of strange human, and by the prospect of spending the night in the cage of a strange hamster, he could only cower, shivering. Elsie looked at him and ran back down the curtain.

'It's not hard,' she said, and she stroked his head tenderly. Then she began to nose and nudge him upwards, staying behind him this time in case he lost his grip on the curtain.

Now, as you know, hamsters are not generally very sociable creatures. In most cases it is absolutely essential for them to have a cage to themselves. But there was a special bond between Elsie and George. A hamster's memory, like everything else, can be weakened by harsh treatment and poor diet, so George only had a partial memory of the Time Before. But while he'd been busy eating the scraps beneath the kitchen table, Elsie's memories had been returning. She remembered that the two of them had been the runts of a large litter – the only two, in fact, who had been runty and dark. They had clung together then in order to survive, to get some share of the food and to avoid being picked on, since even their mother (or dam, as they called her) seemed to favour the others. They were the last to be chosen by owners, and in fact had only been taken out of the cage on the day of the Terrible Attack – an event so terrible that even Elsie's memory went blank at that point. But suffice it to say that what she now felt for George was a powerful protective bond; a bond of flesh and blood, bone and whisker, that came from looking out for one another in the earliest days, and feeding one another, and lying curled up together, a little apart from the rest. And she could tell just by looking at George and smelling him that bad things had happened to him since they parted, which made her angry. She had always suspected that humans weren't entirely to be trusted, though her own treatment by Lucy had been exemplary. She had heard dreadful rumours about Thomas's hamster, though, that he had developed Wet Tail from stress, and had to be taken to the vet, so she knew it was wise to be wary. She checked George's rear end carefully as he climbed the curtain but fortunately, though balding, it appeared to be dry. She only wished she could sink her teeth into the humans who had treated him so badly, but for now she had to content herself with helping him up the curtain as well as she could.

At last they got to the top and George found

himself facing Elsie's cage.

Although not quite as impressive as Mabel's, it was more impressive than any George had ever known, and wholly unlike his own. There was a triangular compartment with a wheel attached to the outside, and a food bowl, and a water bottle inside, and this was connected by a long, curling, multicoloured tunnel to two round compartments stacked on top of each other. One of these was, like Mabel's, full of sawdust for burrowing, the other contained another wheel and a climbing frame. And at the very top of these two there was a small circular compartment that Elsie said was her bedroom. She had got out by dislodging the little plug that led to the sawdust chamber, and there was a small heap of sawdust around it on the ledge.

George blinked in awe. He had never imagined a dwelling so luxurious, or fragrant.

'Now, what I propose to do,' said Elsie, in businesslike tones, 'is to keep you tucked away in the sawdust room. I'll sleep where I usually sleep, so Lucy won't get suspicious, and I'll bring you food. And I'll let you know whenever she's asleep or out so that you can come out and exercise. But first – a drink.'

Elsie seemed to have it all worked out, and George couldn't help but admire her plan, though really he didn't like to impose. But he followed her into the wonderful softness and fragrance of the sawdust room, and burrowed steadily until they came to the rainbow tunnel, which led into the triangular dining area, where George drank long and deep from the water bottle. Then there was more food, crackers and bits of malt loaf from Lucy's lunch box, and proper hamster food such as George had hardly ever eaten. George ate his fill and drank some more, while Elsie ran to and from the sawdust chamber taking things she thought he might need in hiding. Then, when he could eat and drink no more, she said, 'Time for bed, I think.'

And only at that point, it seemed to George, did he realize just how exhausted and utterly bone-weary he was. He tottered on his feet as he turned to face the sawdust chamber.

'Steady now,' said Elsie, and she cleared the entrance to the rainbow tunnel for him.

George looked at Elsie and his eyes were big and very bright.

'I can never thank you enough,' he said huskily.

'Nonsense,' said Elsie briskly, though she was feeling more than a little husky herself. 'You get some sleep. But just be very careful not to show yourself, not even a whisker, until I come and give you the all-clear. You'll be quite safe if you burrow far enough in.'

And with that she touched his nose briefly with her own.

'Night night, dear,' she said, and went ahead of him into the rainbow tunnel, making her own way through the sawdust chamber to the activity room beyond.

George burrowed into the thick, soft sawdust. He had never had the experience of sleeping in such luxury before, and couldn't quite get used to it. And now that he was alone, even though he was so tired, he was a little troubled by all the strange sounds and smells. When the family came in he started and trembled, and as Lucy came up the stairs it took all his self-control to keep still. She hunted round her room for quite a long time once she realized she'd left the door open, then started to play with Elsie. The sound of her voice, and the overpowering smell of small human, disturbed George so much that he wanted to run, yet he knew that his safety depended on staying exactly where he was. It was evening, not his natural time for sleeping, and for quite some time he could hear the sound of Elsie on her wheel, or the curtain flapping, or Lucy moaning in her sleep and flinging an arm out, but gradually exhaustion won over fear and he slept deeply for many hours.

Elsie didn't fall asleep for some time. She ran round her wheel for almost an hour after Lucy went to sleep, thinking hard. She was a resourceful creature and enjoyed planning. Her plan depended on the fact that her cage had only recently been cleaned, and since Lucy was a human of regular habits she knew nearly a week would pass before it would be cleaned again. Even so, she knew that what she had undertaken, the care and concealment of an extra hamster, was no small thing. And what they would do when the cage was cleaned she really didn't know. Still, the main thing was that for now George was safe, and food and water weren't a problem because Lucy checked every day to see if they needed topping up. She might be surprised at Elsie suddenly eating so much more, but Elsie hoped she would just keep on filling the bowl. In any case, she reminded herself, they could always supplement their diet by foraging downstairs. 'One day at a time, Elsie,' she told herself, and finally, feeling a little weary after her adventure, she stopped running round her wheel and climbed up through the short tube to her bedroom, where she too fell asleep.

7 The Call

'Frank,' whispered the strange, yet frighteningly familiar voice.

'*Frank.*'

Frank ran up the ladder to his bedroom, then back down again.

'Frank,' murmured the voice.

'Who – who are you?' Frank managed to ask.

Silence.

Frank ran to the bars of his cage, then along them, gnawing furiously.

'Frank,' said the voice, yet again.

'Go – away –' Frank said to it mentally, gnawing frantically at a bar. 'I – don't – need – this.'

'Need,' said the voice. That was all it said, but suddenly Frank gave up chewing and sank down, cowed, his ears flattened against his skull. Then he looked up towards the window, at the tips of the tall, feathery grass. And to the slice of moon beyond, which to Frank's eyes was just a white smudge. Maybe there was even a star, Frank thought, somewhere out there, beyond the range of his eyes. He had always wanted to see a star. If he closed his eyes, he could see them – great open tracts of sky where the stars blazed. When he opened his eyes he could see the window. It seemed to Frank that whatever it was that called him was beyond that window, in the Wild.

'Frank,' it said.

The problem was that ever since his conversation with Mabel, Frank hadn't been able to get the Black Hamster out of his mind. The Dark One, who would lead him to the Pits of Doom. Sometimes he had bad dreams that made him squeak aloud; at other times he simply stood, paws raised, staring forlornly out of the window. It seemed to him that he didn't know what to think any more.

Even Guy noticed that something was wrong. Frank was frequently startled to find Guy's enormous face pressed close to the bars of his cage.

'What's it all about, Frankie?' he would ask. 'What's up?'

But of course Frank couldn't tell him. He couldn't even explain it to himself. He could only nibble without enthusiasm at the cheese and chutney sandwiches Guy offered.

'Frank,' sighed Guy. 'You look as if you've got the weight of the world on your shoulders.'

And indeed that was the way Frank felt. For if the thing you've always wanted, the thing that calls to you, is a bad thing, then what are you supposed to think, or do?

So for the first time Frank made no attempt to get out of his cage, but stood on his platform, staring wistfully out of the window.

Until one night, when it all became too much.

Frank woke from a long, terrible dream. In the dream he was in a warm burrow under the earth, and all around him there was a familiar, comforting smell. He lay curled around the body of another hamster, his mother maybe, or a brother of the Den. Whoever it was, it seemed right and natural to lie that way. But then he came to a point in the dream when he knew that the thing around him wasn't kin. And opening his eyes (though he wanted very much not to see) he saw that the pelt of the other hamster was as dark as night, and he was staring right into Frank's eyes.

'Hello, Frank,' the other hamster said, his lips curling back in a terrible grin. 'I knew you'd come to me in the end.'

When Frank woke up from this dream, he found he was actually sweating in horror. For a long time he remained where he was, sweating and trembling. Then, just as he was beginning to relax –

'Frank,' said the voice in his ear.

Frank practically somersaulted in his bed.

'Frank,' the voice said again, and it began whispering to him, terrible things that he didn't want to hear. So he took chunks of his bedding, and stuffed them, piece by piece, in his ears till, in fact, most of his bed was sticking out of his ears. But then (and this was a truly terrible moment for Frank) he found that *he could still hear the voice*! It was speaking from inside him somehow, from his own blood.

Then at last Frank knew that there was no escape. Worn out by the effort of trying not to hear, he took all the bedding out of his ears and sat still, waiting in a kind of despair.

And then the voice said something else to him, something quite different from all the things it had ever said before.

It said, 'Courage!'

Frank stiffened, and stood as nearly upright as he could, within the confines of his bedroom.

'Courage!' it said again.

Frank had forgotten his motto.

For the first time in days Frank left the platform where his bedroom was and trotted down the ladder to the floor of his cage.

The room was dark and Guy was nowhere about. But there was the window, and there, luminous and hazy to Frank's eyes but bigger, it seemed, than he had ever seen it before, was the moon.

And looking at it, Frank knew.

Frank knew that whatever it was, this thing summoning him, his own instincts or a thing of evil, he had to face it. He had to follow it and track it to its source. Even if that source happened to be the Pits of Doom.

Once he knew this, everything became clear. He ran up the bars of his cage, and easily chewed through the wire Guy had knotted round the entrance for extra security (poor Guy seemed to have forgotten that rodents have teeth), then he pushed the cage door back as he had done before and finally emerged, a free hamster!

From then on it was easy to run along the ledge to the gap behind the fire, and drop through the gap on to the wooden joist, and from there to the floor beneath the floor, and the darkness and dustiness and mustiness of the Spaces Between.

And there he paused. He knew he didn't want to run along the joist to the chink he'd found before that led to Mabel's front room. He didn't want to explore the inside of the houses at all. No. What Frank really wanted was to make his way outside somehow, to the Wild, where the tall grasses waved beneath the moon. He ran, first one way then another, coming to a row of bricks that seemed to have no outlet or chink through which he could possibly burrow. He turned a corner and ran still further, until he began to feel that he was lost.

There was a bad smell from somewhere, and following it cautiously Frank came to a dark patch of oily water. And here, between a brick wall and a fetid pool, he was finally brought to a halt.

I'm trapped, he thought, and for the first time it came to him that he could die there, in the dark, unnoticed, without ever finding his way to the Wild.

Perhaps this was what Mabel meant by the Pits of Doom, he thought suddenly, and then he thought what a fool he was, and that he would die a fool's death in the dark, by the stinking water.

Then even as he thought this, another smell arose, not from the water itself, but close, and not just the smell of rotting, airless things, though it did smell of age and neglect. There was another note in it too, wild and strange.

Even before Frank raised his eyes, he knew what he would see: a deeper blackness outlined against the dark, but with a reddish gleam around the eyes and teeth: the Black Hamster of Narkiz.

'Hello, Frank,' he said.

8 George Learns His Lesson

Meanwhile, Elsie had been training George. She had demonstrated to him several Techniques of Proper Grooming, including a short course on keeping his droppings out of his food, and woke him up regularly for exercise sessions. She explained everything about the house and family to him, especially about the Boy in the Roof, who must at all costs be avoided.

On the whole, her plan of hiding George in the sawdust chamber worked very well, and as Elsie grew more confident she allowed George out more often, while she stayed in her bedroom. There were only two instances when they came close to being found out. One was when Lucy woke unexpectedly in the middle of the night to find both wheels running round furiously. She half sat up, staring at the cage in sleepy amazement, but fortunately she wasn't really awake and soon turned over and lay back down. The second incident was more serious, and involved the Boy in the Roof.

Lucy once again had forgotten to lock her door, and Thomas came bursting in like a thunderclap. It was George's turn to exercise on the climbing frame, and he froze as Thomas bounced towards him. Every bad memory he had of Jake and Josh returned with terrible force. Inside her bedroom, Elsie froze too. Would Thomas take one look at George and realize it wasn't Elsie? There was no chance at all that he wouldn't look in the cage, because Thomas was very jealous of Lucy's hamster, and she guarded the cage so fiercely that he wanted all the more to break into it and handle Elsie. So now his eyes lit up when he looked at the cage and saw that a hamster was in it, alert and ready to play.

Straight away his large, freckled face loomed over George.

'Elsie!' he cried, and George backed away, terrified. He ran towards the sawdust chamber as

the lid came off the activity room, but the next moment Thomas's hand was in the sawdust, groping around.

'Come on, Elsie,' he said, as George ran into the rainbow tube. 'Eh – what've you done to your tail?'

Because there was still a bald patch just above George's tail, though the hair was growing back.

'What've you done?' repeated Thomas, and he pulled the tube apart.

George leaped across open space to the dining area, but Thomas snatched and caught him by the rear.

What might have happened then I really don't know, but at that moment Lucy returned, and gave a howl of outrage as she realized what was going on.

Thomas let go of George, who ran to Elsie, and there followed so much yelling and shrieking and flying of small objects around the room that Elsie and George could only cling to one another very tightly and hope for the best.

Lucy drove Thomas out.

'And don't come back!' she shouted. 'She's *my* hamster.'

'Well, you ought to take better care of her then,' Thomas yelled back. 'She's going bald!'

'Rubbish!' said Lucy. 'You don't know what you're talking about.'

'Oh no?' said Thomas. 'Take a look then – near her tail.'

'OUT!' said Lucy as he tried to get back in.

'I'll show *you*.'

Elsie let go of George.

'Oh no, Elsie, don't,' he quavered.

'I have to,' she whispered back, 'or she'll take the lid off.' And she ventured nervously down the tube to the activity room.

'Come on then, Elsie,' Lucy murmured. 'Let's have a look at you,' and she picked Elsie up as she left the tube and examined her carefully.

'*See*,' she said, holding her up to an astonished Thomas on the other side of the door. 'There's nothing wrong with her. You just made that up to get a closer look, didn't you? Well, take a good look now because that's the last time! You can get out now and stay out – *out* – OUT!'

Elsie cowered at all the shouting. But Lucy locked the door again and petted her, then put her back while she reassembled the cage and scooped up the spilled sawdust.

After this, Elsie took good care that only one of them was visible at any one time, and that whenever the children were around, Elsie was the visible one. And you must remember that Elsie and George looked really quite alike, especially as George's pelt improved. Girl hamsters are bigger than boys, but Elsie was quite small anyway, and their colouring was similar, so you could only tell them apart if you saw them together, and Elsie made sure that didn't happen. She also made sure that George was fed well, and always gave him the greater portion of food. Lucy had been very surprised to find that Elsie suddenly wanted twice the usual amount, and once checked her over carefully to see if she was getting fat, or even having babies, but since Elsie didn't seem to have changed, she simply gave her more food whenever the bowl was empty, as Elsie had hoped.

So George was properly fed for the first time in his short life, and well exercised. But best of all was the sleep. After the disturbances of the first night he had slept profoundly, through the rest of that night and all the next day. He hadn't woken up until the middle of the following night, refreshed as never before. It was the first time he had ever slept without fear of being rudely awakened by either Jake or Josh, and after four more days of rest and food and exercise he already looked a different hamster. Fur began to grow over the bald patches, his whiskers were no longer tangled and drooping, and it was possible to see in him the confident, handsome hamster he might once have been.

Elsie knew, however, that he was still haunted by terrible fears. She heard him squeak aloud in his sleep, and twist and struggle through his dreams. She put this down to his sufferings at the hands of Jake and Josh, knowing nothing of his other, worse nightmare. He had told her something of his time with the two boys, and she had listened, appalled.

'Why didn't you bite them?' she asked.

'I did try to nip,' said George.

'I don't mean *nip*,' said Elsie. 'I mean, draw blood.'

Elsie could see that George needed General Confidence Training.

'You have to show them you're not afraid,' she said. 'It's all in the way you stand. Like this –'

And she reared up into a hamster's most threatening pose, showing her abdomen, puffing out her cheeks, and baring a splendid set of teeth. George quailed.

'And then if you really need to scare someone off,' she said, 'you do this.'

And she got into the same pose again, this time emitting the hamster War Cry – a volley of aggressive squeaks.

George somersaulted backwards in terror and hid in a pile of sawdust.

'George? What's the matter? George! For goodness' sake, come out,' said Elsie, hauling him out of the sawdust by the scruff of the neck. 'What am I going to do with you? You can't let people bully you all your life. Because if they can,' she said darkly, dusting him off, 'they will. But at some point you have to say, "Enough!" And show them who's boss. Who is boss, George?'

'You are, Elsie,' George squeaked.

'No, George – not me – you! You are the boss. Say after me –'

And she made George repeat several times that he was the Boss. Then she set about teaching him the Threatening Stance.

'Feet apart – like this – legs stiff – back straight – that's better. Doesn't that feel better, George?'

'Not really, Elsie,' said George meekly.

Elsie tutted.

'Now, George, look,' she said. 'Look at me. This is something you have to do. No one else can do it for you. You have to stand up for yourself. You – have – to – do – it.'

She said it so earnestly that finally George, who up till then had been thinking things like, 'Oh all right then', and, 'It's all right for you, you've never had to put up with rough treatment', began to see that in fact he did have to do it. And that only he could do it. And even that he might just possibly be able to.

'Now,' said Elsie, brushing a few more specks of sawdust from his pelt. 'Try again.'

So George reared up as far as he could, which

wasn't very far because he really was a very undergrown hamster, and squeaked as loudly as he could. The effect was rather more comic than frightening, but to her credit Elsie didn't laugh.

'Not bad, dear,' she said. 'But you forgot to puff out your cheeks – that's very important. And keep your feet wide apart – like this.'

So Elsie carried on coaching George, because at the back of her mind was the thought that he really couldn't stay there for ever. By Elsie's reckoning it was only two more days to the Grand Cage Cleaning that occurred once a week, regular as clockwork. And then George was sure to be discovered. They might hide him, of course, in another part of the room while the cleaning went on, they might even get away with it once or twice, but it was impractical to think that they could go on concealing George for ever. One wrong paw, one second out in their timing, and Lucy would find him. And while it was just possible that she would keep the two of them, Elsie felt that the risks were too great. For one thing, if there were two hamsters in the house, Thomas would almost certainly claim one of them, which would be just as bad as sending George back to Jake and Josh. Or Mrs Keenan might insist on taking George to the pet shop, where he would be bought by someone else, and they would never see one another again. Or there was an even worse possibility (and Elsie knew about this because of the terrible fate that had befallen Thomas's hamster) – they might take him to the Vet, where he would be Put to Sleep. Elsie shuddered at the prospect.

Of course the most likely outcome would be that Lucy would simply take him back to Jake and Josh, because she would have heard, by now, of their loss. Elsie had thought of this as well. If he had to go back, she thought, then it would be better if he went back voluntarily. And so this was what she was preparing him for, the best way she could. She intended to tell George this at some point, when he was stronger, but she hated having to break such bad news to him when he was getting on so well, and she didn't know how.

In the end, George himself saved her the trouble. One day, when she had just finished demonstrating the Lightning Twist Propulsion

Manoeuvre (the same one that Frank had used so effectively on Guy), she noticed him looking at her in an odd sort of way.

'What is it, George?' she asked.

George said nothing for a moment, then he said, 'Elsie, why are we doing all this?'

Taken aback, Elsie murmured something about Assertiveness, and General Life Training, but George said, 'It's because I have to go back, isn't it?'

Elsie wanted to protest that he didn't have to go anywhere, he could stay with her for ever, but she couldn't bring herself to lie to him.

George stared into the far distance. 'Yes,' he murmured, 'I have to go back.' And his shoulders drooped in a way that wrung her heart. She knew that she too would be saddened by his departure, and would miss him very much, but she didn't say anything, because she also knew that he was facing up to the inevitable in the way that a hamster can. After a long pause, George turned to her.

'Right,' he said. 'What next?'

Elsie wanted to hug him for his courage, but

something in his bearing made her stand aside.

'We'll try the War Cry again, shall we?' she said. 'Put your shoulders back – right back – that's it – and blow those cheeks out – really blow – good. Now show your teeth – excellent – now let's hear that cry –'

'SQUEAK!' said George.

Inwardly Elsie sighed.

'That's much better,' she said. 'But you need to push more from the diaphragm – and you'll feel a kind of wriggle in your throat when it comes. Let's give it another try, shall we? Feet apart, and blow those cheeks out –'

They tried and tried until they were both quite tired, and finally Elsie said, 'That'll do for today, George dear – we'll try again later on. It's nearly morning now,' and she turned towards the tube that led to her bedroom, reflecting sadly that George still seemed to have a long way to go.

But suddenly George felt that he didn't want to give up. He stretched up as far as he could go, stiff-legged, and thrust his abdomen forward. Then he blew his cheeks out further than he had ever blown them before. It felt most peculiar, yet somehow right. Then he took a breath that seemed to swell his whole body. His diaphragm kicked in, he felt the muscles of his throat contract and –

'*George!*' gasped Elsie, spinning round. 'George, you've got it!'

She clasped her paws to her face, thrilled. 'That was it, George – that – was – it!'

George deflated to his normal size. He could feel that he had gone a little pink round the nose area, from exertion and embarrassment, but he couldn't help smiling.

'It was, wasn't it?' he said.

'*George,*' Elsie breathed again. 'Oh, George – that was splendid.'

And George cuffed her playfully, and she cuffed him back, and they rolled around in the sawdust making little happy chirruping noises that weren't quite squeaks. Then Elsie fell serious, and said solemnly to him, 'You know what this means, don't you, George dear?'

George combed the sawdust from his whiskers and looked at Elsie.

'It means you're ready,' she said. 'Oh, George – you're ready.'

George felt a pang, then a hollow, sinking feeling, but he knew she was right. They had both thought through the options and come to the same conclusion – that he couldn't go on hiding for ever. So now they both felt that they should waste no time, and together they made their plans. The thing was, Elsie said, to get plenty of sleep that day in preparation for the journey. Then George should take all the food he could pack into both pouches, to keep him going. George pointed out that it wasn't really very far, but Elsie said you never knew. Then they talked about what he might do if he ran into the Cat.

As she talked Elsie became aware that George was looking more and more downcast. His ears were flattened, his whiskers drooped. Elsie too felt a peculiar feeling in her stomach, as if there was a hole where the food should be, and finally she ran out of things to say.

George was looking at her in a forlorn way that tugged at her heart.

'I wish I didn't have to go,' he said.

Elsie looked away.

'Well,' she said quietly, 'it's not for us to choose, is it? Our lives don't belong to us in that sense –'

But here her voice became a little shaky, so she stopped and blew her nose on a scrap of bedding.

'Well,' she said again, 'we really must get some sleep –'

'Will I ever see you again?' said George.

Elsie couldn't look at him. The words she expected herself to say ('Of course you will', 'We'll stay in touch', and 'I'll visit') died away on her lips. Because in truth she didn't know. While quite adventurous in her own territory, she had never in her life left the house before. She had dim memories of having heard terrible stories about Spaces Between, and even if she negotiated them there was the Cat, and the dreadful boys. Now as they stood together, she suddenly felt quite certain that in fact they would never, ever meet again.

George reached forward and touched the tip of his nose to the top of her head.

'I'll miss you,' he whispered.

Elsie raised her head and looked at him.

'Oh, this is ridiculous,' she said. 'I'm coming with you.'

George blinked. 'What?' he said.

'I'm coming with you. You can't possibly go all that way on your own. Anything could happen. We'll pack enough food for two and set off as soon as the family are asleep.'

'But you can't come with me,' George said. 'What about you? You'll have to go all the way back on your own.'

'If you can do it, I can,' said Elsie stoutly. 'I don't want anything to happen to you.'

'Elsie,' said George. 'I don't want anything to happen to *you*.'

Elsie began to be very busy, scrabbling around in the sawdust for spare food.

'Well,' she said, 'I'm not leaving you alone. So we'll just have to take that chance.'

That night, when all the household was asleep, Elsie opened the door of her cage. She looked back over her shoulder at George, asking without words if he was ready, and he nodded.

Then she stood back. It was George's turn to lead the way.

Down the canvas curtain he went, across the carpet, through the narrow opening of the door and along the landing. Gurgling noises came from the first door they passed, and raucous snoring from the second, but George trotted along in a determined way until they came to the banister. Here Elsie took the lead, because getting down the rail was considerably harder than getting up. Twice George nearly lost his nerve, but Elsie went slowly and kept encouraging him with cheerful words, till finally they got to the bottom end of it and George climbed off rather clumsily, using Elsie's back as a footstool again.

From then on it should have been easy. All they had to do was to cross to the other side of the room where the vent was, squeeze through, trot across a small section of the Spaces Between and emerge into the meter cupboard in Jackie, Jake and Josh's front room. And they were just about to do this, smiling encouragingly at one another, when suddenly, terrifyingly, all the lights went on, and there was the heavy clunk of human feet on the stairs.

Temporarily dazzled, George and Elsie could only cling to one another in shock. The next moment there was an ear-splitting scream.

'Rats!' howled Mrs Keenan, and seconds later Mr Keenan came thundering along the landing and down the stairs towards Elsie and George.

'Get the shovel, Angie!' he yelled.

At last George and Elsie were able to move.

As Mr Keenan fell over his enormous feet and flew down the last few stairs, roaring horribly, George ran in one direction and Elsie in another, then recovering herself she ran after George. There were cries and shouts from the top of the stairs as the children got up, and the next moment Elsie squeaked aloud as an immense shovel landed on the carpet just behind her. Then they were on the kitchen tiles, heading for the gap between the washing machine and the kitchen units. George paused for breath behind the washer, but the next moment it was pulled out, and Mr Keenan was shouting, 'A stick, Angie – I need a stick.'

Behind the kitchen units George and Elsie

scuttled, across tiles thick with grease and fluff, but Mr Keenan pursued them, dismantling the cupboards as he went by pulling the chipboard away from the bottom so that he could see underneath. George began to think all was lost, when suddenly he came to the pipe behind the sink. The pipe was set into the kitchen wall with mortar, but here and there the mortar had come away in chunks, and there was a hole big enough for two frightened hamsters to scramble through. Hesitating for only a second (he had no idea what was on the other side), George was then forced to leap upwards to avoid the shovel as Mr Keenan slammed it under the sink, narrowly missing Elsie. He pushed and kicked and wriggled into the hole, hoping against hope that Elsie would follow.

'Angie, get the chisel!' shouted Mr Keenan. 'And the plunger!'

George pushed and struggled some more, then fell into a kind of gap, and a moment later Elsie landed on top of him with a soft thud. Above them was the sound of a hammer, and a shower of mortar cascaded down, then Lucy's voice rose above the general racket.

'Mum – Dad – stop it! It's not rats – it's Elsie!'

Elsie and George picked themselves up and ran along the inside of the gap behind the sink. They were in total darkness, and there was a lot more mortar to scramble through. Elsie, panting and wheezing, didn't seem at all her usual self.

'Oh – oh dear,' she gasped. 'I – don't – know – when – I've – ever – been – so – frightened.'

George didn't either, but he was saving his breath. It was hard work clambering over all the rubble, and the dust was getting into his eyes and up his nose till eventually he had to stop because he could hardly see or breathe. He sneezed several times and Elsie bumped into him, sneezing too.

'George dear,' she said, as they got their breath back. 'Where are we?'

But George didn't have the faintest idea.

9 The Black Hamster of Narkiz

Frank stared at the Black Hamster, and the Black Hamster stared back at Frank. Fear and something else – recognition? – lifted all the fur on Frank's pelt, yet he couldn't run. He stood, paralysed. Run, said his blood, but his limbs couldn't move. And something deeper told him that running was useless. About a hundred things that he might usefully say flashed through Frank's mind, but in the end all he said was, 'What do you want me to do?'

In answer the Black Hamster simply turned and set off in a different direction. Frank felt compelled to follow, and he scampered after as fast as he could, paws slipping from time to time on the fine rubble between the joists. He couldn't help but notice that the Black Hamster never

seemed to slip, and made no sound at all.

Soon he also noticed that attached to the joists above him, and running perpendicular to them, was a pipe. The pipe was covered in a strange material, thick and sticky, not unlike tar. The Black Hamster seemed to be following this pipe and Frank followed too, though before him rose an image of Mabel's face. Pits of Doom, it whispered with a feral smile.

Where the pipe met a brick wall it was surrounded by an earthenware container, and a different kind of air blew through this, earthy and damp, with the scent of rotting things inside. With a single look back at Frank, and an expression that was as frightening as Mabel's, the Black Hamster climbed easily inside the clay container. Frank hung back, but he hadn't come this far to give up now, so after a single shudder he followed, into the cold, evil-smelling clay.

The container turned into a clay pipe, chipped in places so that water came in, forming a slime on the bottom. The next few moments Frank would rather forget, as he slipped and slithered after the Black Hamster, who was always just too far ahead for Frank to catch up.

'Oh, where is he taking me?' Frank moaned inwardly, but soon found that there was no time even to think; all his energies were concentrated on keeping up. Here and there he found droppings among the chippings of stone and pot beneath his feet. 'Rats,' he thought, 'or mice.' Or maybe other hamsters that had been Lured. The pipe got steadily dirtier, earth falling through the chinks as well as water and petrol. From time to time there were terrifying tremors and vibrations, and Frank realized with a thrill of fear that they were actually under the road.

If ever Frank needed his motto it was now. Dirty and dripping and entirely lost, this was the moment when he most wanted to give up. Even though he had yearned to be out in the Wild, it was a very different feeling to be actually leaving the territory of the houses. And if the Pits of Doom were anywhere surely they would be here, where his instincts couldn't guide him and all he could do was to follow blindly the dark shape ahead into the unknown.

But if you have a good motto, it doesn't just disappear, and you can't ever really forget it. So now, just when Frank's nerve was about to fail entirely, he remembered the word 'Courage!' and it was as though a little voice had spoken inside him. A voice as distant and faint as one of the stars Frank had heard so much about but never seen. Faint as it was, he couldn't ignore it, and as his faltering steps picked up it was as if his own personal star began to glow.

And so they went on, muddy fluid dripping on them until Frank's pelt was coated with grime. Then the smell became more earthy, and Frank noticed worms wriggling through the chinks. Though very tired now, Frank also felt a glimmer of excitement, thinking of the feathery, waving grass that had beckoned him for so long.

Ahead, the Black Hamster paused and raised his nose, then began to burrow upwards, out of the pipe and through one of the cracks, and Frank followed, struggling through wet earth. It had been a wet spring, and the earth was as unlike the Syrian sands as it was possible to be but, even so, older instincts seemed to be returning and telling him what to do.

The smells around him were richer and more varied than any he had previously known: earthworm, beetle, and many different kinds of root. There were droppings too, left by voles and mice. Frank pushed on, pausing only briefly to examine a snail (something told him that in other circumstances he might eat it), and finally he emerged into a place where tall grass grew so thickly he could hardly see, and a multitude of new smells assailed his nose. They made his flesh tingle and his blood stir, and at last he knew he was where he had always wanted to be – in the Wild.

Somewhere ahead of him the Black Hamster pressed on through thick grass, and Frank followed, though he was deeply distracted by all the different scents and the tiny animals that scuttled past. He felt more alive than he had ever felt, and stronger, with all his senses working at once.

Gradually the grasses thinned and they came to a clearing. Frank glanced upwards and quickly crouched, because the black sky blazed with light.

'Stars,' he breathed.

As you know, Frank had never seen stars before, and now he thought he must be dreaming, for they seemed so near, so shiny, and so real. For all his blurred vision he could still see the depth and brightness of the sky.

A moment later all the brightness was blotted out as the Black Hamster reared up above Frank. He seemed much bigger, and Frank crouched still further before him, waiting for the blow, and the grip of teeth.

'If I die now,' he thought, 'at least I will have seen what I have seen and smelled what I have smelled,' and he rolled over in an attitude of submission.

But the blow never came. Instead, the Black Hamster did a most unexpected thing. Folding his forepaws on his chest he bowed deeply before Frank, almost touching the earth.

Frank raised his nose in surprise. And he saw the Black Hamster raise his own nose and cry aloud, a wild and melancholy call. Frank scrambled to his feet, and saw ...

... thousands of hamsters, vast crowds that stretched in all directions without end!

Without being told, Frank suddenly knew that he was looking at the whole of the Ancient Tribe of Hamster, from the beginning of time to the present day.

Then the Black Hamster began to move. Keeping his forepaws folded, he extended his left foot towards Frank while turning slowly on his right. He stepped sideways, continuing to turn in a circle, now spreading his arms wide, the palm of his right paw facing up and his left down. Frank felt a shock of recognition. Mabel's dance, he thought.

But before he had time to think this through, he saw that as the Black Hamster moved the whole Tribe of Hamster moved with him. Following his steps they turned slowly in unerring motion, lifting their voices with his in a wild and melancholy refrain.

Frank listened, enthralled. Though the song had no words he understood it. He knew he was listening to the history of the hamster race; the song of its belonging to the earth, and its final separation from both habitat and tribe. Frank was thrilled by the music, then as he listened, he knew he had to follow.

Tatty and matted as he was, Frank rose and folded his forepaws on his chest. Tentatively he extended his left foot, then soon he too was moving round and round with all the others of his race, following steps he seemed to know from a long time ago. He found it easy to fall in step with the others, as though they were moving to the drumming of his blood. He turned with them as they began to spin, expecting that at any moment he would get dizzy, or lose his balance, but each time he completed a revolution his eyes met the eyes of the Black Hamster, and they seemed to smile into him and keep him strong and sure. Once or twice they passed each other, and were so near that Frank couldn't help himself: he stretched out a paw and felt, beneath a soft thick pelt, a warm, beating heart. 'Flesh and blood,' Frank thought, remembering what Mabel had said. The Black Hamster was as real as he was, if not more real. And he glanced up shyly to see if the Black Hamster minded being touched, but the bright, brave eyes only laughed into Frank's; he seemed to be full of joy. Then the next steps sent Frank spinning away.

Round and round he twirled, with all that vast company of hamsters, and at last he knew the full power and glory of his tribe.

And just at that point all the hamsters fell to the earth, prostrate. Frank lay with them, shivering with delight and realization, and what he felt went beyond words.

Then, gradually, as he lay for what might have been a long time, the light began to change, and Frank felt the cold. Slowly he raised his nose and sniffed. Stiffly he clambered to his feet.

There was no one around – no one. Not one of the thousands of hamsters remained. Worst of all, there was no sign of the Black Hamster.

For several moments Frank ran around, sniffing behind stones and the thicker stems of plants, as if it might just be a game, and they might all be hiding.

'Don't leave me,' he called to them. 'Don't go.'

But there was nothing, and no one. Frank was entirely alone, on the wild heath, under a strange sky!

When this realization dawned, Frank stood absolutely still for several moments, not knowing what to do. Then a flutter of darkness above reminded him to dive for cover behind an old tin can, and a second later an owl swooped and rose with a mouse squeaking in its claws.

That brought Frank to his senses. He had forgotten what a terrifying place the Wild could be. He wasn't safe here and he had no idea where to go. But when another owl screeched above him he cowered and then he ran, in and out of the grass and stones and the sharp objects he found among them: tin cans, a broken bottle, an old ball of rotted rubber, and a paper cup still containing tea, which Frank lapped at though it wasn't very appetizing, because he was beginning to feel both hunger and thirst.

Now that the other hamsters had gone, the night was full of noise. The rumble of a train that made the ground beneath him quake, the wail of a siren, and, worse than these, the occasional screech of an owl, or yowl of a cat, for Mrs Timms' cats were out hunting, rustling the grass. Combined with the sudden sense of being lost and alone, these noises reduced Frank to a quivering terror. He could hardly think, but ran blindly. His nose was filled with the stench of petrol and cats. The cats seemed to be all around him, and in his panic he was losing his sense of what to do.

Tired and miserable, Frank began to wonder if this was what Mabel had meant by the Pits of Doom. He had been lured to the Wild, granted a glorious vision, then abandoned to the night. Utterly lost, he was rapidly entering that state that any rodent knows and dreads – a kind of terminal confusion, in which everything around seems so alien and frightening that you forget, not only how to act, but who you are.

Then he stopped running. What, after all, was the point? He was just about ready to give up entirely when the grass in front of him parted and a greyish nose peeped out.

It was a mouse.

'Who are you?' it squeaked.

Frank was silent.

The mouse came closer and sniffed.

'Who are you?' it said again, and its voice was strange to Frank. It spoke with the accent of the Wild.

'I don't know,' he said at last.

The mouse trotted round him. 'You don't belong here,' it said. 'Where've you come from?'

'I don't know,' Frank said again.

'You don't know much,' said the mouse, trotting round him the other way. 'Well,' it said. 'You don't belong here, that's for certain.' It paused, considering, then had a sudden thought. ''Ere,' it said, 'you don't come from the Houses Beyond, do you?'

Frank said nothing, but his memory stirred.

'I went there myself once,' the mouse went on. 'Nasty, dusty, smelly places – full of cats. Lucky to escape, I was. But if you live there then that's where you live. You don't look to me like you'd survive out here. How did you get here though – no, don't tell me – you don't know.'

'No,' said Frank.

'But you think that's where you've come from? A room somewhere – bright even at night – and a hand that feeds you?'

Frank vividly remembered Guy.

'Yes –' he said.

'I thought so,' the mouse said, pityingly. 'You're one of them. Born and brought up in a cage.' The mouse shuddered. 'Well – you'll have to go back, of course. You'll never survive. Once a caged animal always a caged animal.'

At these words Frank felt a bitter despair and his nose drooped to the ground.

'Now don't get upset,' the mouse said kindly. 'Tell you what – you're in luck. If it's them same houses you're not far off – I can show you how to get back there.'

What else could Frank do? He followed the mouse through a clump of nettles and a thicket of brambles, and a place where shards of glass glittered in the moon.

'Mind out,' said the mouse, skipping nimbly past. Frank did his best. He couldn't help but admire the assured way the mouse moved and seemed to know its way about the Wild.

Gradually the stench of petrol grew stronger, though the road was quiet now, except for the rattle and clatter of a milk lorry that sounded horribly loud in the silence. Soon the grass cleared and they emerged into a bright place beneath a lamp post. The mouse took cover behind a stone.

'This is the place,' it said. 'If you cross here, in a straight line, mind, you'll come to a little metal flap in the pavement – like a half circle. Drop down that and you're in the clear water drain. It's a bit wet but you'll manage – and it goes right back into the house. Make sure you get the right opening – any of the others and you're in trouble – don't go down no grids. It's the only one with a cover like a flap. Just follow the pipe.'

'Aren't you coming?' Frank asked.

'No fear – this is as far as I go. You won't catch me in no houses again,' said the mouse. 'Still – if you've been brought up to it I dare say you don't mind the smell. Though how you put up with the cats I don't know.'

'I don't live with the cats,' Frank said, remembering.

'Coming back to you, is it?' said the mouse. 'That's good. You'll feel a lot better once you're home. Now the road's quiet and you'd best set off before any of the Big Machines come. Straight across, mind – no turning off. Good luck. The names Capper, by the way. Capper Fieldmouse.'

And he was off, before Frank had time to thank him.

The thought of going back was appalling to Frank. Going back, after all he had seen and experienced. To a *cage*. How on earth could he live in a cage now? On the other hand, how on earth could he live out here? Frank knew in his heart and bones that the little mouse was right. He had no choice. He couldn't survive in the Wild.

It was a despondent and dispirited hamster that first set paw on the great stretch of glittering tarmac that divided the Wild from the Houses Beyond. By the time he was half-way across, it began to seem like a very great road indeed.

Frank felt horribly exposed. What if a cat saw him, or an owl, or the Big Machines came? Once he thought he saw a cat's eyes, eerily lit by the light from a lamp post, but it was now the still hour before dawn and no cars passed. Part of his mind thought that he shouldn't even mind if one did roar by suddenly and flatten him, but his feet went on trotting and his luck seemed to be in. Once he had clambered up the kerb the smell of houses was stronger than the smell of the road, and Frank found the metal flap easily. It did lead to a disconcerting drop down a wet pipe, into shallow water, and it might – who knows? – take him straight to Mrs Timms, where all the cats were. Despite these dark thoughts, Frank's deeper instincts surfaced, and he kicked and paddled through the water until the clay pipe ended at the wall of the house. There, Frank dropped down through a gap in the brickwork and knew that he was once more in the Spaces Between. There was no immediate sign of a joist, but to his right there was another pipe, like the one he had left his house by so long ago, it now seemed, when he had followed the Black Hamster into the Wild. This time he was alone, more alone than he had ever felt in his life, as his memories returned with the familiar territory. Still, he felt there was no choice but to go on, and he squeezed himself into the clay pipe above and began trotting along it, back the way he had come.

10 The Worst Fear

'Well, where do you *think* we are, George?' asked Elsie.

George sniffed the air miserably.

'I don't know,' he said.

After falling into the space behind the sink, they had trotted along a narrow corridor between bricks for what seemed like hours. Elsie clung to George. Here, in this rubble-strewn passage, she was a different hamster. George could feel her shivering and knew that she was experiencing, for the first time in her life, what any hamster experiences when taken away from its territory: a loss of confidence, and an inability to think. He didn't like to say that he thought they were lost, so he kept pushing forward in as confident a way as possible, in the hope that it would make her feel brave. But they had passed a stretch of wall through which there was a strong smell of cats, which had unnerved George too, then another stretch which was damp and piled high with mortar, and still there seemed to be no way out of the passage. Now George's confidence had ebbed, and he didn't know what to say.

In fact they were travelling through the cavity, the space between the inner and outer walls that ran right along the terraced row. They had passed George's house without knowing it, and Mrs Timms', and they couldn't find a single outlet or opening that would take them to the spaces beneath the floor, or simply allow them to change direction. They could only go forward or back, and as George couldn't see that there was any point in going back he pressed on.

Then at last there was a space, a missing

brick. Joyfully George pushed his way through it and found himself sliding down in the rubble, beneath joists. He followed the joist and came to yet another brick wall, at the end of which there was a corner. There was a pipe above them and the floor beneath them was damp and soiled.

'George?' Elsie said fearfully, but he didn't answer.

'Which way, do you think?' she said.

Silence.

'Take your time,' she quavered. 'Do you need a rest?'

'No, Elsie,' said George at last. 'I just don't know where we are.'

'You must recognize something,' Elsie urged, but George could only shake his head.

Elsie was silent. Perhaps she thought that by not saying anything she would give George a chance to remember something about the Spaces Between, but in fact it only made him more nervous. He stared into the darkness of the turning of the way.

'I – I think it's this way,' he said, and he took a few steps forward, then stopped.

'I don't know,' he burst out miserably. 'I've no idea.'

Elsie stared at him as the implications of this sank in.

'Oh George,' she said, after a moment. 'Whatever are we going to do?'

When George didn't answer she said that maybe they should just pick a way, any way, and follow it. 'We can't just stay here,' she said. 'We'll never get out. And then the B—'

Elsie couldn't bring herself to say the words. She swallowed and tried again.

'The Black Hamster might come,' she whispered.

Both Elsie and George knew about the Black Hamster. They had been told about him as babies; how he lured safe hamsters away from their homes, and when hamsters were lost and alone in dark places, he came. This had been the unspoken fear in the back of their minds all the time they had been travelling through this unknown territory, and now Elsie had spoken it. George didn't know what to say, but he felt he should say something. He licked his lips and was about to answer, when suddenly they both froze.

'*What was that?*' squeaked Elsie in a whisper, clutching George, and they both listened, horrified, as a scrabbling noise came towards them along the pipe. Nearer and nearer it came, then the pipe itself seemed to quiver and bulge.

'The B–Black Hamster,' Elsie stammered out, but she seemed unable to run or even move, and could only cover her eyes as a wild and shaggy form nosed its monstrous way from the pipe above.

'Hello,' said Frank.

Elsie couldn't speak or even look, but George surprised her very much by thrusting her behind him and assuming a defensive stance.

'Who are you?' he managed to say, in a clear if high-pitched voice.

Frank shook himself and oily fluid flew everywhere.

'I'm Frank,' he said. 'Who are you?'

He advanced towards them, sniffing, and both George and Elsie cowered back.

'Frank,' said George. 'Not – not – the Black Hamster?'

Frank paused mid-sniff.

'The Black ... what do you know about the Black Hamster?' Frank asked.

Elsie peeped out from behind her paws.

'The Black Hamster,' she said, 'is he from whom all evil comes – the Source of Darkness – the Scourge of all our race. It is he –'

'So not very much then,' Frank interrupted, quite rudely, but before Elsie could reply, George said, 'If you're not the Black Hamster, who are you, and where have you come from?'

Frank sat back on his haunches and began to wash his face and ears.

'I've already told you my name,' he said, between washes, 'but I don't remember you telling me yours.'

Something in the homeliness of this gesture disarmed the other two, and Elsie took her paws away from her face.

'I'm George,' said George, 'and this is Elsie.'

Frank went on washing, unperturbed, as they drew near.

'Do – you – have – an – owner?' Elsie squeaked, as if addressing someone foreign and slightly deaf.

At the word 'owner' the strange hamster drooped a little, and no longer seemed quite so frightening.

'Yes,' he said in a voice just above a sigh. 'Yes, I have an owner.'

'Where is he then?' Elsie asked, braver now. 'Where have you come from?'

Frank told them. He could see that they were astonished and impressed and a little dismayed to hear that he had been outside, beyond the boundaries of the houses, in the Wild. He tactfully left out the details of the Black Hamster, sensing from their earlier reaction that they weren't ready for this kind of information just yet. He could sense also that they weren't the adventurous kind, so he couldn't quite work out what they were doing here, in the Spaces Between.

'What about you?' he asked. 'What brought you here?'

In turns they told him the full story. Frank bristled when he heard about George's mistreatment at the hands of Jake and Josh, and thrilled at the story of their escape.

'And now we've found one another,' said Frank. 'What amazing luck!'

Elsie and George looked at each other.

'Well, actually,' George said, 'we're lost. We're rather hoping you'll be able to show us the way back.'

'Back?' said Frank. 'Why on earth would you want to go back?'

Elsie and George looked at him.

'You think there's no alternative, don't you?' Frank went on. 'But there is. Hamsters weren't born to live in cages, you know. There is a world out there — a world you can live in — I've seen it.

Oh, I know one hamster couldn't survive alone, but two or three could – we could start a tribe!'

His voice rose in excitement as he saw the possibilities, but Elsie interrupted.

'I don't want to live out there, thank you very much,' she said. 'I want to go back home.'

'Home?' Frank said. 'You mean – to a cage?'

'What's wrong with that?' said Elsie. 'I've got a very nice cage, thank you.'

'But it's still a cage!' Frank said. 'You still have no idea what it's like to be free – to live on the open earth – to see stars!'

Before Elsie could reply, George asked, 'What is it like?'

'It's wonderful,' Frank said with emotion. 'You've no idea – it – it's as though – there – you can be who you're meant to be.'

Elsie shuddered. 'Whatever made you go?' she said.

Frank hesitated. 'A – voice –' he said at last.

George and Elsie huddled together again.

'A – voice?' repeated George.

'I knew I had to follow it,' Frank said slowly, 'Or go mad.'

Elsie and George exchanged worried looks.

'What kind of voice?' George queried huskily.

'It led me to the Spaces Between,' Frank said dreamily. 'And on and on until I thought I was hopelessly lost. And then –' Here Frank took a deep breath, because he knew how what he would have to say would sound. 'I saw him. He appeared.'

George moistened his lips with his tongue. 'Who?' he managed to ask.

'The Black Hamster,' said Frank, and Elsie gave a little cry and hid her face in her paws again.

'He's not like that,' said Frank earnestly. 'I've heard the stories too – he's not like that at all. He – he showed me things that I'll never forget –'

But here his voice trailed off, because he felt he would never be able to say what he had seen. Elsie and George continued to look at him fearfully.

'I thought that if you saw the Black Hamster,' George said, 'that you were lost. I thought that he took you straight to the Pits of Doom.'

'Yes,' said Elsie, 'no one survives seeing him.'

'But I'm not in the Pits of Doom, am I?' said Frank patiently. 'I'm here, talking to you.'

'Why did he let you go?' said Elsie.

'He didn't "let me go",' said Frank. 'He – disappeared.'

'What – and left you all alone?' said George.

Frank nodded, feeling again the pain in his heart from being left.

'Well, that doesn't make any sense,' said Elsie. 'Why would he go off like that and leave you?'

This was a question Frank still couldn't answer, and suddenly he felt very tired.

'You haven't got any food on you, have you?' he said. 'I'm starving.'

In fact between them Elsie and George had quite a lot of food on them, and they hadn't eaten any of it yet. When Frank said he was starving, they both realized at the same time how hungry they were, and they set about extracting the food from their pouches to share it with Frank.

When they had all eaten substantially, George said, 'What I don't understand is, how all these houses link up.'

'That's easy,' said Frank, and he told them what he knew about the terraced row, and where their houses must be in relation to his. It took them a little while to establish the details, but soon they had the territory roughly mapped out, with Elsie's and George's houses at one end and Frank's at the other. Frank told them about Mabel, next door to him, and George told Frank about Mrs Timms and her many cats.

'We don't want to end up there,' he said, shuddering.

None of them knew whether there were any other houses, but Frank began to think that it might be interesting to find out, to explore this territory at least, since it seemed unlikely that he would convince either Elsie or George to follow him into the Wild.

'I wonder whose house we're underneath now,' he said, as if to himself. He looked at Elsie and George, then back along the joist. 'There's only one way to find out,' he said.

'But what if we are under Mrs Timms's?' said George.

'That's a risk we'll have to take,' said Frank.

'It seems like a big risk to me,' said George.

'Well, we can't stay here much longer,' Frank said.

'No, but –'

'Courage is my motto,' said Frank.

'Good for you,' said George. 'I dare say you've never met a cat.'

Frank was about to reply when Elsie said, 'He's right, George dear, we can't stay here for ever.'

'If it was the house with all the cats,' Frank said reasonably, 'we'd surely be able to smell them.'

George was silent, remembering that they had, in fact, smelt them from the cavity, but had gone past.

'Do you know how to get out?' Elsie asked.

'I think so,' said Frank, and he told them what he knew about joists, that they ran up to the walls between houses, and where they met the wall there was usually a chink that a hamster could get through.

'It seems to come out by the skirting board,' Frank said. 'And if it is the wrong house, if there is a cat, we'll definitely be able to smell it by then.'

George still had misgivings, but Elsie was so anxious to be out of the Spaces Between that finally he gave in. Frank led the way and Elsie followed, George bringing up the rear. And soon they came to the end of the joist and there, just as Frank had predicted, was a tiny crack. Frank jumped up immediately and began pushing and squeezing himself through, and Elsie followed. George hung back a moment, still haunted by nameless fears; but he certainly didn't want to be left alone in the Spaces Between, so he steeled himself, and as Elsie's back legs disappeared he too jumped towards the crack.

As soon as Frank pushed his way through he knew where he was. He was in the bright pink, deep pile carpet he recognized from the time before, and the smell of hamster was even stronger

now. He was in Mabel's house, but he didn't want to spend any time talking to Mabel, who would understand even less than Elsie and George about the Black Hamster. No, Frank was interested now in exploring the territory beyond Mabel's, even if it meant accompanying Elsie and George all the way back to their cages. At least it was a Project, something he could do rather than return to his own cage and to Guy, so he pushed his way through the carpet, intent on getting to the other side of the room. His efforts cleared a path for Elsie, who followed with only a little difficulty through the thick, dirty pile, but after a moment she stopped.

'Where's George?' she said. She raised her nose and sniffed, then turned before Frank could stop her, and retraced her steps.

A wholly unexpected sight met her eyes.

George was snout to snout with an enormous white hamster. He was cowering in the Submission Pose, paws raised as though convinced of attack. Mabel was looking at him with a ferocious smile, and when she saw Elsie her smile widened.

'Well, well, well,' she said. 'How nice to have company.'

11 Mabel Versus George

'Perhaps you've popped by for dinner?' Mabel suggested mildly, but her eyes gleamed.

Elsie was speechless. Powerful and shocking memories were returning. Frank made his way over to George.

'Leave him alone,' he said. 'What have you done to him?' For George was cowering and trembling in the most abject way.

'Oh, it's you again, is it?' Mabel said. 'I thought you were off looking for your friend – the Black Hamster.'

Frank wasn't going to rise to this.

'What's the matter with him?' he asked again.

Elsie knew.

The moment she had seen the dazzling white hamster she knew what her sense of smell had already been trying to tell her, and now she was experiencing almost as powerful a memory as George. A memory of being a cub again; one of two rather neglected cubs from a large litter presided over by a large, white and unpleasant dam.

Yes, George and Elsie were Mabel's cubs.

You should know that normally hamsters are very good mothers, even though they can litter when very young, like Mabel. They look after the largest litters scrupulously when it comes to feeding and grooming, for the first few weeks at least. After that, well, it can happen that they fail to recognize their own cubs, and at that point they have to be separated. Also, if the mother is disturbed when looking after her young, they should be separated. Because, unpleasant as this may sound, if a mother hamster (or any maternal rodent for that matter) feels threatened, she may attack and even try to eat her babies. No one knows why this is. Some people think she may be trying to put them back into her body to keep them safe.

And now you can probably guess the source of George's worst nightmare.

Once Mabel had given birth, Tania only managed to persuade her mother not to take her back to Mr Wiggs' pet shop by promising to find homes for all the babies. And so a continual stream of Tania's schoolfriends visited the cage, looming over the babies with many oohs and aahs. The cubs were kept in the cage until old enough to leave and, as they got older, Tania's friends wanted to handle them as well. The fine white hamster babies soon found homes, but no one seemed interested in Elsie or George. The children took them out and played with them, not roughly but a little too long, and when Tania put them back the smell of strange children on them was overwhelming.

The rest, for George, was the stuff of his nightmares: the rush of teeth and claws, the huge, suffocating body over his. Most fortunately, Elsie managed to raise the alarm by emitting the sharp little volley of squeaks she had demonstrated so effectively to George, and Tania's father lowered his newspaper.

'Good heavens!' he cried. 'She's eating the babies!'

And he managed, at some cost to his own fingers, to prise Mabel's jaws apart.

That was it. Homes had to be found. Even though it was one of the many periods in which Tania and Lucy weren't speaking, Mr Wheeler took Elsie and George round to Lucy's house in a box.

Fortunately, for Elsie at least, Thomas's hamster had just died, and both children begged their parents for another one.

'Thomas had the last one – it's not FAIR!' shouted Lucy, for once at a greater volume than Thomas, and finally her parents said that they supposed the cage was there to be used. But they didn't think that Thomas was quite ready yet for proper hamster care, and they wouldn't be moved on this point, so Thomas stamped up the stairs to his room in a sulk.

Lucy was very definite. She didn't mind having a brown hamster, in fact she quite liked the fact that it would be a different colour from Tania's, but she did want a girl, and she didn't want the damaged one. So Elsie found a home, but of course it was George that Mr Wheeler was worried about, and so in a last-ditch attempt he called on Jackie. Mrs Wheeler never spoke to Jackie if she could help it, but Mr Wheeler was desperate.

'Oh, poor little thing,' said Jackie. 'Oh – go on, then.'

So now you know why there were so many

hamsters on Bright Street.

And you know the full story of George's Terrible Traumas – the reason why now, faced with his worst nightmare, he could only cower and quake, while Elsie trembled also, with fear and anger, and Frank gazed at them all, mystified.

'What's the matter with him?' Mabel said in response to Frank. 'I haven't the faintest idea.'

She stepped forward and gave George a rather brutal nudge with her nose.

'What's eating you, eh?' she asked, and poor George fainted clean away.

Elsie squeaked in alarm and Frank hurried over to prop George up and pat his cheeks and paws.

'Well, for heaven's sake,' said Mabel, amused. 'Whatever's the matter?'

'You should know,' snapped Elsie, glaring, and Frank said, 'Hang on, he's coming round.'

Elsie held George's head and stroked it tenderly, but as soon as he opened his eyes and saw Mabel again he shrieked, 'No, no!' and wriggled frantically, and passed out once more.

'Oh, George, George,' moaned Elsie.

'Dear me, what a fuss.' said Mabel.

'Will somebody tell me what's going on,' said Frank. 'Do you three know each other?'

'You could say that,' said Elsie quietly. 'She's our dam.'

'That's right,' said Mabel, and her eyes lit up with a carnivorous glow. 'I'd quite forgotten.'

'Your – dam?' said Frank in astonishment.

Elsie looked darkly at Mabel. 'Look,' she said to Frank. 'He's coming round again. Let's move him a bit further away, shall we? From *her*.'

'Oh, don't mind me,' Mabel said, preening herself with the same amused expression. 'This is only my domain, after all.'

Between them, Frank and Elsie got George to his feet and moved him a little way through the thick carpet. George still couldn't bear to look at Mabel, but once they were a few inches away he managed to stand by himself.

'So – she's your *mother*?' said Frank incredulously, in low tones.

'Yes,' said Elsie quietly, then raising her voice a little she said to George, 'Are you feeling a bit better now, dear?' and George rested his head on her shoulder.

'Well – but –' said Frank, 'what happened – I mean –?'

'She tried to eat him,' said Elsie shortly, and George buried his face in her shoulder and moaned.

Frank looked at them both in horror.

'It's rude to whisper,' said Mabel suddenly and all three of them started in alarm. She had crept closer to them while they had been attending to George. Elsie recovered first.

'I was just explaining,' she said with a hostile glare, 'that when George was a baby, you tried to eat him.'

'*Eat* him?' said Mabel scornfully. 'It was barely a nip.'

'I was there, remember,' said Elsie loudly. 'They had to pull his head out of your mouth.'

Frank said slowly, 'You tried to eat your own baby?'

'I really don't remember,' said Mabel loftily. 'It was all so long ago.'

'You remember all right,' cried Elsie hotly, but Frank interrupted.

'I thought you said that it was hamsters in the

Wild that ate their young,' he said.

'Did I?' said Mabel, with great nonchalance.

'Come on, Frank,' said Elsie. 'We should go.'

'Yes, do go,' Mabel said. 'You're invading my territory.'

'No, wait,' said Frank. 'You said a lot of things,' he went on. 'Not just to me, but to Elsie, and George. About the Black Hamster.'

Elsie and George drew their breath in sharply and Mabel blinked.

'All that about the Pits of Doom,' Frank went on, getting louder. 'About luring hamsters to their death, derangement and disease. Was any of it true? I don't think so.'

'What would you know about it?' hissed Mabel. She wasn't smiling now.

'Rather more than you, I expect,' said Frank, 'since I've just been with him – in the Wild!'

There was a shocked silence, then Mabel gave a little, fluttering laugh.

'What nonsense,' she said. 'Don't be ridiculous.'

'You don't believe in him, do you?' Frank said incredulously, advancing towards her. 'And yet you said all that – to me and Elsie and George.

Making him out to be some kind of a – *monster* –
and you don't even believe he exists!'

'Of course he doesn't exist,' snapped Mabel.
'He's a warning, that's all. A warning to foolish
hamsters who might otherwise wander off. To
teach those of us who don't know any better to
stay in our places.'

'Stay in our places?' Frank echoed. 'Stay in
our places? Is that all you can say? We had a place
once –' he said, turning to Elsie and George, 'we
had a home out there – in the Wild –' He waved
his arms expressively. 'We had *so much* – and now
all we have is a cage!'

'Fool!' hissed Mabel. 'Hamsters like you
would undo all the progress we have made. You
would return us to a life of Danger and
Deprivation! All on a whim – a fantasy about a
life you've never known. You would give up
security and provision, and return to being Prey!
You're nothing but a Renegade!'

'And you,' shouted Frank, equally furious, 'all
your talk about security – and progress – you had
nothing to do with it. You're nothing but a – a –
Mutant!'

And now at last Mabel reared up, displaying her splendid white abdomen and ferocious teeth. She was far bigger than Frank, and would have descended on him with all her weight, but then a most unexpected thing happened.

It was George – *George* who ran between them and held them apart!

'S-stop it – b-both of you –' he stammered out.

Sheer surprise caused both Frank and Mabel to pause.

'This isn't g-getting us anywhere,' George went on. 'T-time's g-getting on – and we don't know when the B-Big Humans m-might appear. And m-me and Elsie would v-very much like to get home b-before that happens.'

Frank glared at Mabel and Mabel glared at Frank. Then slowly Mabel sat back on her haunches.

'You should listen to the little pipsqueak,' she said. 'He's got sense if he hasn't got guts.'

Frank looked as if he might rise up again at this, but Elsie placed a restraining paw on his arm.

'Let's go,' she said.

'Let me show you the way,' said Mabel, and she waddled ahead of them, round a chair. After a moment's hesitation Frank followed with Elsie and George. There, a little way ahead, was the skirting board on the opposite side of the room.

'Don't let me keep you,' she said.

Frank, Elsie and George filed past Mabel. Mabel kept her eyes on George the whole time, and just as he was next to her she smacked her lips loudly and said, 'Yum yum!'

'Stop it!' Elsie cried, and Frank said, 'What kind of a mother are you?'

But George, instead of fainting again, stood a little straighter than before and walked past his mother, actually looking her in the eye. And it was Mabel who was the first to look away! But she soon retaliated.

'I don't know where you think you're going,' she called after them. 'There's no way out – if he's told you there is, he's lying. And even if you get past the next house, there's the one after that where the cats are –'

This was actually quite useful information, of course. Frank and George and Elsie kept their heads down and took no further notice of Mabel, but they explored all the way along the skirting board without finding a single crack. Frank tugged and pulled at strands of carpet to get a look at the floorboards beneath, but without success.

'What did I tell you?' Mabel said smugly. 'And now, if you don't mind, I'll be getting back to my nice warm cage. See you in the morning.' And she ran a little way up the chair.

'You'd like that, wouldn't you,' Frank said. 'Well, we won't be here in the morning but you will – and every morning for the rest of your life! You'll never see any more of the world than you can see from your cage – you'll never know what it's like to be free –'

Mabel yawned ostentatiously, patting her mouth with her paw.

'Oh, go back to your cage, Squeaky,' she said, and she ran up the rest of the chair and disappeared.

Stung, Frank was trying to think of a sharp reply when Elsie said, 'Look,' and she pointed towards the corner of the room where there was a piano.

The back of the piano stood against the skirting board, but at the top of the skirting board there was a gap, between the back of the piano and the wall, large enough for a hamster to squeeze through. It was a desperate plan, but it was their only hope. George climbed on Frank's back and squeezed through.

'It's all right,' he called to the others. 'There's plenty of room,' and so Elsie clambered up and through, then she stood on George's back and helped to pull Frank through the narrow space.

There was far more dust and fluff here, at the back of the piano, than in the main room, and they all sneezed and coughed as they nosed their way about, looking for gaps.

'Here –' George spluttered at last. 'I've found one – over here!'

There in the very corner, where the carpet ended and where the floorboard joined the skirting board, there was a tiny hole. So small that they actually had to nibble at it before they could get through, but soon it was big enough for first George, then Elsie, then Frank to wriggle down and drop into the Spaces Between.

'I've been thinking,' said Frank, once they were all safely down on the floor beneath the joist. 'It ought to be possible to travel all the way under the floor without coming up into the houses and running the risk of meeting any cats.'

'Well yes – it is,' said George, and he explained to Frank how he and Elsie had travelled along the space between walls, that seemed to run the whole length of the terrace.

'Yes —' said Frank, and he started to scrabble. 'But there ought to be some way — somewhere under one of these joists — yes! Look — a hole here — at the bottom.'

Elsie and George gathered round while Frank showed them the new crack he'd found.

'If I go through here, instead of up there,' he said, 'I should be able to travel under Mabel's front room rather than through it — to my house, which is on the other side — you see?'

Elsie and George saw.

'So it should be possible to do the same when we go the other way, to your houses,' Frank explained triumphantly. 'That way, no risk of cats — we just climb out when we want to — in George's house, then Elsie's.'

He looked at them expectantly. It was a brilliant plan.

There was a pause. Elsie and George looked at one another.

'What do you mean, "we"?' George said at last.

'Isn't your house the other way?' said Elsie.

'You'd be going a long way out of your way,' said George.

'You'd be much better off going home,' said Elsie.

Frank looked from one to the other of them.

'But – I don't want to go home,' he said.

Elsie stepped forward and placed a paw on his arm.

'Frank, think,' she said gently. 'What will you do once you've seen the two of us back home? You'll have to go back sooner or later – and it's a long journey to make without food. You've done so much already, Frank,' she said as he started to speak. 'Don't think we aren't grateful. But it's too dangerous to risk going all the way with us and then all the way back again. We can't possibly let you. It's above and beyond the call of duty.'

'But, I don't mind danger –' Frank began, but George said, 'Elsie's right. There's no point taking unnecessary risks.'

Frank's nose and whiskers drooped. He had really begun to think that after his disappointment and sense of failure in the Wild, he had found a new adventure – maybe, even, the beginnings of a tribe. Elsie and George weren't much of a tribe, but they were better than nothing, and while there were three hamsters rather than one, he felt there were more possibilities. But now it came to him forcefully that Elsie and George didn't want to be part of a tribe, or have adventures, they didn't really want anything other than to return home.

Frank looked so forlorn that, unexpectedly, Elsie reached forward and kissed his nose.

'Sometimes it takes more courage to live with what you've got,' she said.

She had said the magic word, 'Courage!'

'We won't forget you, Frank,' she said, and George came up too and said that they'd never forget.

Frank was touched. He felt that the three of them had made a kind of bond, even if they weren't a tribe. He still didn't want to go home, but he could see the sense in what they said. There was no point in taking unnecessary risks.

'We will stay in touch, won't we?' he said, and both Elsie and George said that of course they would. And he could visit them once he had proper supplies, now that he knew the way.

Frank could see that it was time to leave.

He burrowed a little way into the crack he'd found.

'I can feel the floor,' he said. 'It's quite easy – you shouldn't have any trouble –'

Then, before going through, he turned and raised a paw to them in salute, not sadly, but with a smile that said, 'Keep it up!' and 'Courage!' Then he was gone, disappearing into the crack in the wall.

12 George Wins Through

There isn't much more to tell. Elsie and George followed the main joist until they came to the next wall. There, without too much difficulty, they found a hole under the joist and wriggled through to the space beneath the floor of the next house. Here the smell of cats was so overpowering that they knew they were actually beneath Mrs Timms' front room, and that the next house they came to would be George's. At the next wall they came to, therefore, they looked for an opening at the top of the joist so that George could get into his front room, and here again they found one easily enough, but George paused before going through.

'I'm just a bit worried about the cat,' he said. 'It should be all right – he usually sleeps upstairs

– but still – no harm checking.' And he pushed just his head and shoulders through and sniffed.

A moment later he withdrew his head quickly and dropped back down.

'It's no good,' he said. 'He's there. I knew he would be somehow – I don't know how – I just knew.'

He shook his head. Elsie stared at him in dismay.

'But, George,' she said, 'what shall we do?'

George frowned.

'Well,' he said. 'I do have a plan, because I was half expecting this to happen. But it's dangerous, and a bit desperate.'

George's plan was that they should confuse the cat by appearing at different times. While he ran after one, the other would appear in a different part of the room and distract him. They would take it in turns to run from one item of furniture to another. George reckoned that the cat was not a particularly intelligent animal and would never understand that there was more than one of them, particularly since Elsie and George looked so alike.

'I don't like asking you to do it, Elsie,' George said, looking worried, 'but it does mean that you'll get back into your house without having to be on your own in the Spaces Between. The trick will be getting him to run after me while you get back through the meter cupboard into your own front room.'

Elsie sat back on her haunches and looked at George with shining eyes.

'George,' she said, 'you are clever, thinking all that up on your own.'

'Well, but there are risks,' said George. 'And I don't want you getting hurt, Elsie.'

Elsie's eyes were misty.

'Oh, George,' she said, 'I will miss you.'

George said that he would miss her too, and they nuzzled, knowing it might be the last time. There wouldn't be a chance at the other side of the room after all. George would get back to his cage as fast as he could, Elsie would head towards the meter cupboard. So now Elsie groomed George behind his ears, and told him to remember everything she'd said, about grooming himself, and keeping his droppings out of his food

165

bowl, and most of all about Looking Fierce and Biting Hard. George said nothing, but lifted his nose to hers and stroked underneath her chin. Then, when there was nothing at all left to say, George squeezed himself through the narrow chink and set off running.

Sergeant lay curled on the flowered settee, apparently asleep, but as soon as George started his ears pricked, then his tail twitched, then he was up and bounding off the settee towards George.

This was Elsie's cue to run towards the settee as George whisked himself under it. Sergeant came to a sudden halt, braking with all four paws at once. He looked first one way then the other, then, losing sight of George, bounded towards Elsie.

'Coo-ee,' called George, as he crossed from the settee to the lamp. 'Here I am,' and Sergeant wheeled round so quickly he almost fell, and Elsie ran from the settee to the chair.

'No, here,' she called from behind the chair legs and Sergeant turned again, then when George called him from between the legs of a giant robot, Sergeant ran round and round after his own tail.

This gave George time to get to the dresser next to the table on which his cage stood. The legs of the dresser were twisted and easy to climb, and it would be simple, George reckoned, to get to his cage from the top. Meanwhile Elsie made it all the way to the meter cupboard (the doors of which never shut properly, you will remember, because of the carpet).

Then suddenly, just as George made it to a drawer handle that was nearly level with the table top, Sergeant made a great leap and landed on top of the dresser.

It was a terrible moment. Elsie's heart was in her mouth as she peeped out from between the doors of the meter cupboard. Sergeant was ready to pounce whenever George moved from the handle of the drawer.

Faced with almost certain death, George did a very brave thing. Relying on the techniques taught to him by Elsie (specifically the Lightning Twist Propulsion Manoeuvre, in which, if you remember, all the muscles contract at once,

propelling the hamster forward), George leaped.

It was a leap such as a flying squirrel might have been proud of: all the way from the drawer handle to the table top. Unfortunately, at almost the same moment, Sergeant leaped. But – and here all the hamster gods must have been with George – Sergeant missed!

Whether he caught his paw in the flex of the lamp that stood on top of the dresser I can't say, but he tumbled off the dresser, rocking it violently and taking the lamp with him. George, meanwhile, scuttled up the bars of his cage to the entrance.

Sergeant squalled horribly as he fell and Elsie covered her eyes, then got ready to run to the hole at the back of the cupboard in case he came after her. But Sergeant was no longer interested in pursuit. He stalked off in an offended manner, shaking his front paws, and when Elsie peeped out from the doors of the meter cupboard again there George was, clutching the bars of his cage and looking for Elsie.

'Oh, well done, George, well done,' Elsie squeaked. 'You were marvellous.'

George went pink.

'It was nothing,' he said modestly. 'I rather enjoyed it, in fact.'

Then he pressed his face to the bars.

'Goodbye, Elsie,' he called. 'Take care.'

And Elsie knew that the time had come.

''Bye, George dear,' she squeaked in a whisper, then before Sergeant had time to change his mind, she whisked herself out of sight and went to find the hole in the back of the cupboard.

George didn't have time to feel too desolate. For one thing he was starving, and he still had a bowl of food in his cage that Jackie had left for him in the hope that he would return. For another, the noise of Sergeant's fall had evidently alerted Jackie, and George had hardly started to eat when he heard her footsteps on the stairs, followed, far too quickly, by both boys simultaneously tumbling down.

'It's that mad cat again,' she said, and she went to pick up the lamp. Then, 'George!' she exclaimed, and the next few minutes were an uproar as the boys yelled in excitement and fought over who should hold him first. But Jackie lifted him just out of reach.

'I told you he'd come back,' she said happily. 'Where've you been, little fella?'

'Let me hold him, Mum, *please*,' begged Jake, and George was passed first to Jake and then Josh.

'Steady now,' he told himself, to calm his nerves. But he didn't feel as frightened as before. In fact, in many ways he felt a different hamster. He put up as well as he could with the children seizing him and passing him from one to the other and shouting his name. He had come back to these people, he told himself, and somehow he had to find a way of living with them. Even so, it was getting a bit much for him, especially when Josh dive-bombed him in and out of his cage, making a noise like a bomber plane.

'Now that's enough,' Jackie said, and George heartily agreed. 'He's come back to you two – goodness knows why – and I only hope you'll treat him a bit better this time.'

She took him away from them.

'Nice to have you back, little fella,' she said, running a finger from his forehead to his tail and lowering him back into his cage. 'You get some sleep now. And you two,' she went on, turning to Jake and Josh, 'look at you! You're a disgrace. Get upstairs and wash your hands and faces. It's nearly time for school.'

There was bedlam as Jake and Josh fought over clothes and school books, had a fight with their pump bags and tried to turn the telly on (Jackie unplugged it), but finally they were ready and Jackie got them out of the door. Then George spent a quiet day sleeping and eating until they returned, bringing Alex and Jamie, and Khalid from the next street, and Thomas from next door, all to see George.

First they passed him from one hand to another, then Josh put him down the neck of his jumper so that he ran down the sleeve, then up Thomas's sleeve, then they all stood round to see if they could get him to go up and down their sleeves in an unbroken circle. When they were bored with that game they made bridges and tunnels for him out of railway track and the cushions on the settee, then Jake picked up his paint-blaster gun, just as he had done once before.

'Do you think I could fire him from here on to that cushion?' he said.

George remembered everything Elsie had told him. He stood as tall as he could on top of the railway tunnel, blew out his cheeks and bared his teeth in the most alarming manner.

Unfortunately, at that precise moment Jake wasn't watching. He scooped George up and the sound of George's best War Cry ever was drowned as Josh tipped over an entire tub of toys.

'There's a target in here somewhere,' he yelled.

Standing Tall and Looking Fierce had failed George entirely. There was only one option left. Wriggling so that he faced the soft pad of Jake's first finger, George took a deep breath and sank his teeth so far into the flesh that they met.

Jake made a noise like a sports whistle. Unfortunately for George, he also flung his arm about. George held on for a second or two, gripping with his teeth, then he flew through the air in a perfect arc, fortunately hitting the cushion that had been propped up for him. He lay there, winded, as everyone yelled at once.

'Poor little thing,' said a voice George recognized as belonging to Lucy's brother, Thomas. 'It's not his fault. You scared him.'

'He BIT me,' yelled Jake.

Thomas carried George over to his cage.

'I had a hamster once,' he said, sadly. 'But I didn't treat him right and he died. If you don't want him,' he said, 'I'll have him.'

For a moment George's heart beat wildly with hope, then Jake took him off Thomas quite gently and lowered him into the cage.

'Nah,' he said. 'He'll be all right, won't you, George? Let's find something else to play with.'

And they left him alone! Jake sucked his finger quietly as he went away. And from that day on, they treated George with more respect. Just as Elsie had said they would.

Elsie herself got back safely and without incident to Lucy's room. When Lucy woke that morning the first thing she saw was Elsie's small brown face peeping at her from the open cage. And Lucy, who had hardly slept all night since Elsie disappeared, was so relieved to see her that she burst into tears.

She lifted Elsie on to her pillow and fed her with the crumbs from a biscuit she had sneaked up the night before. Elsie was surprised to find how pleased she was to be back after her big adventure. She ran along Lucy's arm and nuzzled her fingers, and let Lucy make steps for her by putting one hand in front of the other.

Then Lucy heard her mother's voice calling her.

'Wait there,' she said to Elsie, placing her back in her cage, and when she returned she was carrying a large roll of tape. To Elsie's dismay, she began sealing all the exits and entrances to her cage, round the joins on the plastic tubing, where one section of cage joined another, and even round the lid.

'Don't worry,' she told Elsie, 'I'll still take you out for exercise. I'll just have to re-seal you every time, that's all.'

Elsie's ears and whiskers drooped. While not really interested in escaping, she did like to forage now and then, and she had been planning to visit George, but now it didn't look as though she'd ever get out again. She would just have to hope that he managed to visit her, though suddenly, somehow, he seemed much further away than before.

Once Lucy had gone, Elsie spent some time reorganizing her cage and making a new place for her bed. She was pleased to be back, warm and clean and safe, with a supply of delicious food that Lucy had brought up specially for her, but for the first time in her life she missed having company. She tucked herself up in her new bed, thinking of George. But Elsie was a sensible, domesticated hamster, and after a long sleep she soon re-adjusted to the regularity of the old routine. And if she dreamed about George occasionally when she slept, and thought about him as she trotted round her wheel at nights, she was also practical enough to know that the dangers that lay between them were great, and to hope that he wouldn't take unnecessary risks. And she had very pleasant memories of their time together which helped her to settle in.

So that was what happened to Elsie and George. But I expect you'd like to know what happened to Frank.

13 **What Happened to Frank**

Frank had plenty of time to think about the Black Hamster on the way home but all he came up with was questions. Who or what was he, and why had he taken Frank all the way into the Wild just to leave him there, knowing that Frank couldn't survive? He remembered all the terrible things Mabel had said, and felt that he'd been a fool to listen, but on the other hand he did feel that he'd been treated badly, and left without guidance. What was he supposed to do with his new knowledge and understanding of the true nature of hamster? Yes, he had met Elsie and George, but they didn't want to know, and now here he was, heading back to life in a cage, just as if nothing had happened.

If the Black Hamster had shown up at that

moment Frank would have had a thing or two to say to him, and he even paused for quite a long time in the Spaces Between, hoping against hope that he would show up. But nothing happened, and it was a tired and forlorn little hamster that finally made his way back to Guy's front room. It was a bright morning, and the sun was already burning down on Frank's cage.

Guy, of course, was beside himself with joy.

'Frank!' he cried, 'Oh, Frank, Frank!'

And for a long time he didn't say anything else, but waltzed round the room, cradling the struggling Frank in his cupped hands, and planting great wet kisses on his head.

'Oh, Frank – I really thought I'd lost you this time! Where've you been, old son? What've you been doing? What've you been up to, eh?'

And he carried on asking Frank questions, 'Just as if I could answer him,' Frank thought, giving Guy an old-fashioned look.

Finally Guy put Frank back in his cage, still talking to him. He brought him fresh water and food, and watched for quite a long time as Frank washed himself and sorted out his bedding.

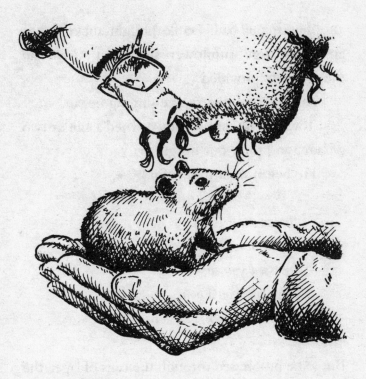

'I really missed you, Frank,' he said.

Usually Frank would turn away from the ugly sight of Guy's pitted, bristly face, the great hairy holes that were his nostrils, but this time he stared back. And for the first time he noticed something other than the ugliness, and the fact that Guy was the Enemy, one of the race that had caged his own; he noticed how very much the human in Guy needed company.

'He isn't *all* bad,' Frank thought, tucking into an extra large sunflower seed that Guy had thoughtfully provided.

But then, of course, the singing began.

Towards lunchtime Guy opened a can or two of lager and took out his guitar.

He began on a mournful note.

> *'Fraaank,*
> *You'll never know*
> *I missed you so;*
> *I thought you'd gone*
> *But you're back, old son ...'*

But as he progressed through the cans of lager, the songs became more cheerful.

> *'Franky*
> *If I wrapped you in a hanky*
> *You'd look just like Widow Twanky...'*

On and on it went, until Frank got so cross he could have rattled the bars of his cage. He tried going to bed and wrapping his bedding tightly round him, but it was no use. In the end he got up and glared at Guy (who wasn't even looking his way), and thought 'Stop!' at him. 'For pity's sake, stop!'

And then an astonishing thing happened.

Guy stopped playing the guitar, mid–note, and said, 'Oh well, that's enough of that,' and put his guitar away!

Frank could hardly believe his ears. He stared at Guy as he wandered into the kitchen. He could hear him moving around. He didn't understand what had just happened.

It hadn't happened, he told himself. It was just coincidence.

Guy wandered back with a couple of cheese and chutney sandwiches (it was still a bit early for a full stack). He sat in front of the television and switched it on.

'How about a nice bit of sandwich, Frank,' he said, proffering one.

'Not chutney,' Frank thought with a shudder, but he prepared to take the offering anyway.

'I don't think you like chutney,' Guy said, withdrawing it. 'Look, here's a nice bit of crust.

No chutney on that.'

Frank sat back on his haunches. Whatever was happening? Had he acquired some strange new power over Guy?

He decided to test this idea.

'The sun's burning directly on my bed,' he thought at Guy and, without even turning to look at Frank, Guy got up and pulled a curtain across.

'You know, I've been thinking,' Guy said to Frank. 'You do get a lot of sun just there. I think you'd be better off a bit further along.'

And he moved first the telly, then Frank's cage, further along the ledge.

Frank didn't know what to make of this at all. He didn't even know how to think about it. 'Surely not –' he thought, and then, 'What –?' But he was too utterly baffled to finish the thought.

One thing was clear, though. The new position of his cage was better. He still had a view out of the window, but he was no longer in direct sun. And Guy had stopped singing, and he had nice clean bedding waiting for him, fresh and warm.

What he needed to do was sleep. After a good long sleep everything would be clearer, and he would be able to put all his adventures into perspective. It seemed to Frank that he had only just realized how very tired he was after everything that had happened, how much in need of a good day's rest. He paused to pick up a few more sunflower seeds before retiring.

'Sleep,' he thought.

'I expect you're off to sleep now,' said Guy's voice, unexpectedly close. 'Well, I'll let you get on with it. I'm off out for a bit, so you can have a nice long rest. Sleep tight, old son,' Guy said to Frank. 'Sleep tight.'